Tri

CW00956814

A PLAY IN TWO ACTS

By Bernard Slade

SAMUEL FRENCH, INC.
45 WEST 25TH STREET   NEW YORK 10010
7623 SUNSET BOULEVARD   HOLLYWOOD 90046
LONDON   *TORONTO*

Brooks Atkinson Theatre

UNDER THE DIRECTION OF THE MESSRS. NEDERLANDER

MORTON GOTTLIEB

Presents

JACK LEMMON

in

TRIBUTE

A New Play by
BERNARD SLADE

with

ROSEMARY PRINZ

TRESA HUGHES   ROBERT PICARDO
CATHERINE HICKS   JOAN WELLES

and
A. LARRY HAINES

Scenery by
WILLIAM RITMAN

Lighting by
THARON MUSSER

Costumes by
LOWELL DETWEILER

Associate Producers
BEN ROSENBERG AND WARREN CRANE

Directed by
ARTHUR STORCH

SETTING

The action of the play takes place in the living room of a New York townhouse and on the stage of a New York theatre.

ACT ONE

Scene 1—The present and a morning three months ago.

Scene 2—That night.

Scene 3—Later that night.

ACT TWO

Scene 1—The next morning.

Scene 2—Earlier this afternoon.

Scene 3—Tonight.

PARTICIPANTS

(In order of appearance)

Lou Daniels—*a chunky, affable New Yorker in his early fifties who looks older than his years.*

Dr. Gladys Petrelli—*fifties, shrewd, maternal and approachable.*

Scottie Templeton—*fifty-one but looks ten years younger. An elegant, charming, pixieish man. A mixture of Noel Coward, the Marx Brothers and Peter Pan.*

Sally Haines—*a beautiful girl in her early twenties.*

Maggie Stratton—*Scottie's first wife. Mid-forties, feminine, intelligent, sympathetic.*

Jud Templeton—*Scottie's twenty-year-old son. Shy, intelligent, awkward and intense.*

Hilary—*a blonde, crisp, well-groomed, attractive woman in her thirties.*

Tribute

ACT ONE

Scene 1

The Time—*The present.*

The Scene—*A New York theatre. A scrim that looks like a front curtain is dominated by an Al Hirschfeld line drawing of Scottie.*

At Rise—*The house lights stay on and the curtain does not rise. Lou Daniels ENTERS and hurries to an area DOWNSTAGE RIGHT. He grins nervously at the audience; shuffles some crumpled envelopes he is carrying; pushes his glasses up the bridge of his nose, peers out to the back of the house.*

Lou. Is everybody in? Is there anybody still out there in the lobby? Good. (*He looks out at audience.*) Would you believe that already I've sweated right through this shirt? Okay, I guess you're all wondering why I called you here tonight. Well— (*He stops, looks up at the back of house.*) Could we have the house lights down? Yeah, we're starting. Could we

. . . The house lights. We're starting. . . . Thank you. (*The HOUSE LIGHTS DIM and multiple rows of LIGHT BULBS on the proscenium GO ON framing the stage. A SPOTLIGHT ILLUMINATES Lou's area but misses him by a couple of feet.*) You want me to move? I can move if you— (*The SPOTLIGHT*

ADJUSTS so that it hits Lou.) Perfect. Now you know why shows go out of town. (*He shades his eyes, squints out at audience.*) You know, now you can't see a damn thing from up here? Anyway, my name's Lou Daniels and I know a lot of you out there know me and some of you know each other and *all* of you know Scottie Templeton. That's why we're all here—to pay tribute to Scottie. (*He mops his brow with his handkerchief, checks notes on envelopes, looks at audience again.*) I was trying to find a way to kick this thing off so I looked up the word tribute. You know, it not only means to pay homage—it also means a gift. Well, that seems fitting because Scottie's given us all a gift—the gift of friendship and the gift of laughter. (*He clears his throat nervously, starts to check his notes, remembers something else.*) Oh yeah, maybe a few people might ask why take over a theatre for one night to give a testimonial to a man who was never exactly what you'd call a household name. Well, there are three reasons—first, Scottie's been stagestruck all his life, second, he has so many friends the only place we could fit them all in was a theatre, and third— (*He grins.*) —Why the hell not? (*He crumples envelopes, stuffs them into a side pocket, thinks for a moment.*) I met Scottie when I was thirteen. Even in those days there was something different about him. For one thing, he was the only twelve-year-old kid I'd ever seen who wore an ascot. Turned out he was going through his Ronald Colman period. Come to think of it, he never entirely got over it. We first met on an elevator. It was jammed with people all facing front, not saying a word as we went from the first to the fifteenth floor. Scottie was the first one off. A few feet from the elevator, he suddenly stopped, turned, held up his hands and said, 'Hold it a minute, everybody! I've got this great idea! Let's all meet a year from today!' I was the only one who laughed and we've been friends ever since. (*The SPOTLIGHT quickly CROSS FADES to pick up* DR. GLADYS PETRELLI *who is standing in an area DOWNSTAGE LEFT.*)

GLADYS. I don't think I'm betraying any professional confidence when I say that for many years of his life, Scottie was the world's greatest hypochondriac. He was also an insomniac. That's a bad combination. Especially if you happened to be his physician. One time, about five in the morning, he called me in a total panic and insisted on meeting me right away at my office. Five A.M.! When I got there, he told me he'd awakened and discovered a dent in his chest. He opened his shirt and, sure enough, he had a cavity right in the middle of his chest. I walked outside, called the night watchman in and asked him to open up his shirt. When he did, I pointed to his chest and said, 'Oh, look, he's got one too! Scottie, *everyone's* got one! Now will you get the hell out of here?' (*Almost imperceptibly the LIGHT on her and the proscenium bulbs start to DIM and we hear a PIANO softly playing a sad, haunting song. We start to bleed through the scrim and the STAGE is gradually ILLUMINATED.*) I could never prove it but I've always suspected Scottie went somewhere for a second opinion. (*We now can see* SCOTTIE TEMPLETON, *wearing a dressing gown, playing the piano in the living room of his townhouse. It is comfortably, tastefully furnished with a slightly raised platform leading to the visible front door, another door leading to the kitchen and a stairway leading to non-visible bedrooms.*) Well, Scottie got over his hypochondria. But you know something? I miss those middle-of-the-night calls. What can I tell you? (*The STAGE is now FULLY ILLUMINATED. The SPOT on* DR. PET-RELLI *is very DIM. She is still talking but we do not hear her anymore.* SALLY HAINES, *a young woman in her early twenties, comes out of one of the bedroom doors and, unobserved by* SCOTTIE, *stands on the landing, watching him. The SPOTLIGHT on* DR. PETRELLI *is now OUT and she is in darkness.*)

SALLY. You write that yourself? (*He stops playing and looks up at her.*)

SCOTTIE. No, that's all wrong. You're supposed to be looking funny but adorable in a pair of my pajamas that are much too big for you.

SALLY. And then my boyfriend comes in, sees me in your pajamas, and thinks we've been to bed together. (*He grins up at her.*) Why *didn't* we go to bed together?

SCOTTIE. Oh, I can explain that. It's the age difference. I'm afraid you're too old for me.

SALLY. I never know when you're kidding.

SCOTTIE. Neither do I. Now, why don't you get your funny little body into the kitchen and bring us some coffee? It's all made. (*She comes down the stairs into the living room, deposits the overnight case she is carrying.*)

SALLY. You're really quite weird. I mean, you charm the hell out of me and then you lure me back to your place and—

SCOTTIE. Now hold it a minute—I've seen luring in my time and last night there was absolutely no luring. Maybe a little *leering* but that's as far as it went. You said the heat was off in your building.

SALLY. You believed that?

SCOTTIE. No. Why'd you say it?

SALLY. You want to hear my philosophy of life?

SCOTTIE. (*Pretending to check his watch—teasing.*) Is this going to take long?

SALLY. I believe in trying everything once. (*She shrugs.*) I'd never been to bed with anybody who was committably insane before.

SCOTTIE. Whatever gave you the idea I was insane?

SALLY. Well, for one thing, the way we met. By the way, where'd you get the doctor's robe?

SCOTTIE. Hospitals are full of them. When did you know I wasn't a doctor?

SALLY. When you wanted to do the internal. I was in the hospital for an appendectomy. What were you in for?

SCOTTIE. Tests, tests. When you're an older person they have to check you every now and then for dry rot, termites, general signs of deterioration.

SALLY. You don't *look* like an older person and you certainly don't act like one.

SCOTTIE. I'll be fifty-one in three months.

SALLY. (*Surprised.*) How'd you manage to look so young?

SCOTTIE. (*Soberly.*) It's very simple, Sally. You see, I've always treated my body like a temple. Never put any alcohol, rich foods—anything or anybody who wasn't totally organic into my mouth. Are you an actress?

SALLY. What makes you ask?

SCOTTIE. The way you're avoiding the kitchen. I've learned the only way you get breakfast from an actress is if you put tape marks on the kitchen floor. (*She grins and EXITS to kitchen but leaves the door open. SCOTTIE softly resumes playing.*)

SALLY. (*OFFSTAGE.*) I'm not an actress—I'm a model.

SCOTTIE. Fashion, photographic or nude?

SALLY. (*OFFSTAGE.*) Make me an offer. Mostly I hand out balloons at conventions. Pretty song.

SCOTTIE. Yeah, maybe someday I'll come up with an ending.

SALLY. (*OFFSTAGE.*) How long you been working on it?

SCOTTIE. About twenty years. (*She RE-ENTERS with a tray of coffee.*)

SALLY. What do you call it?

SCOTTIE. Lack of discipline. (*She looks at him.*) Oh, 'Scottie's Unfinished.' What else? (*She puts tray on table. He moves to pour coffee.*)

SALLY. I couldn't find any orange juice.

SCOTTIE. It's in the bar.

SALLY. (*Looking around.*) Where? (*He points to a spot on the wall.*)

SCOTTIE. Press that secret button under the ledge and you'll be right in the middle of 'Lost Weekend.' (*He pours himself coffee as she presses the button and a small, hidden bar revolves into the room.*)

SALLY. Hey, that's terrific. You sure have a neat place. You a writer?

SCOTTIE. (*Handing her coffee.*) In another life— well, a screenwriter, really.

SALLY. Any I might have seen?

SCOTTIE. Not if you're lucky.

SALLY. You didn't like being a writer?

SCOTTIE. I loved being a writer. I just hated writing.

SALLY. How come?

SCOTTIE. Because you have to be in a room all alone. I like to mix. What I *really* should have been is a head waiter.

SALLY. What do you do now?

SCOTTIE. I'm in public relations.

SALLY. What does that involve?

SCOTTIE. (*He think for a second.*) Actually it's a lot like being a head waiter. (*She grins, checks watch.*)

SALLY. Oops, I have to get to the unemployment office. (*She moves to telephone, writes on pad.*) I'll leave you my full name and telephone number. I'm available for parties, afternoon teas, conversation or almost anything.

SCOTTIE. There's no need for you to rush off, you know. You're welcome to stay and play with me.

SALLY. Thanks, but I'm sure you want to be alone with your son.

SCOTTIE. No, as a matter of fact, the first few hours are usually a bit awkward. (*She picks up a small, framed photo.*)

SALLY. This him?

SCOTTIE. Took it himself. He's always been good with a camera. (*She puts photo down, picks up overnight case, looks at him.*)

SALLY. I want to thank you. I laughed so hard my stitches hurt.

SCOTTIE. Come here and give me a kiss. Right here. (*He indicates his cheek. She moves to him and goes to kiss the spot he's pointing to on his cheek. At the last second, he turns his face so that she kisses him flush on the lips. He grins at her surprise.*) I didn't think a big city girl like you would fall for an old gag like that.

SALLY. (*Grins.*) I didn't. (*She EXITS. He moves up the stairs, closes bar on his way to bedroom. The DOORBELL rings. SCOTTIE REAPPEARS on the landing carrying his suit jacket and tie.*)

SCOTTIE. Come on in, Jud. It's open. (*The front door opens and MAGGIE, carrying a suitcase, ENTERS.*

SCOTTIE, *very surprised, stares at her for a moment. Finally*—) All the gin mills in all the towns in all the world and she has to walk into mine.

MAGGIE. Hello, Scottie. Jud's unloading his stuff from the taxi. (*They look at one another for a moment.*)

SCOTTIE. Well, stop looking up my dress and come here and give me a kiss.

MAGGIE. Why don't you come down here?

SCOTTIE. This is closer to the bedroom. Thought we'd have a little slap and tickle before the kid gets here and puts a damper on everything.

MAGGIE. (*Grinning.*) Could you make that retroactive? (*He comes down the stairs, throws his clothes over the railing and they embrace affectionately.*)

SCOTTIE. You look good, my love. How's that chap you live with treating you?

MAGGIE. That 'chap I live with' is the father of two of my children, has just been made a full professor, and he treats me very well.

SCOTTIE. I'm happy for you, Maggie.

MAGGIE. I know. That's one of your better qualities.

SCOTTIE. What made you fly down with Jud?

MAGGIE. (*Sitting.*) I wanted to visit Dad. He's been confined to a nursing home.

SCOTTIE. I know. I saw him last week. He's a bit shaky, but he's still hanging in there.

MAGGIE. (*Amazed.*) You drove all the way up to Brewster?

SCOTTIE. Well, he is my ex-father-in-law.

MAGGIE. But you never liked him.

SCOTTIE. Yeah—well, I didn't want him to think I just hung around him when I had to. (*The front door is banged open and JUD, burdened down with luggage, ENTERS. SCOTTIE watches him as he has trouble get-*

ting his stuff through the door, stumbles into the room.) How long you been with the Teamsters' union, son?

JUD. (*Puzzled.*) What?

SCOTTIE. It's okay—you missed it, you missed it. (JUD, *still not understanding, nods, deposits luggage.*) How you doing, kid?

JUD. Fine, just fine. (*He approaches* SCOTTIE, *sticks out his hand.*) Good to see you, Dad.

SCOTTIE. (*Not taking hand.*) What the hell is that? Where do you think you are—a Chevrolet dealer's convention? (*Assumes a hearty voice.*) 'Nice doing business with you, Sam.' Now come here and give your old man a sloppy bear hug like a proper son. (JUD *reddens slightly, they embrace rather awkwardly.*) You've filled out since I last saw you.

JUD. (*Somewhat aggressively.*) Yes, but I'm still short.

SCOTTIE. (*Puzzled.*) Do you always walk into a room and make that announcement?

JUD. No, but you haven't seen me for two years and I thought you might be expecting more—growth.

SCOTTIE. It never entered my mind. (JUD *takes off his coat and scarf during following.*)

JUD. Have you told him yet?

SCOTTIE. Told me what?

MAGGIE. A friend of Don's has offered Jud a teaching assistant job for the summer.

SCOTTIE. Where?

MAGGIE. Berkeley. It'll help with his tuition and also be marvelous experience.

SCOTTIE. For what?

JUD. Teaching. I've decided I want to teach.

SCOTTIE. I thought you wanted to be a playwright.

JUD. (*Surprised.*) How'd you know that?

SCOTTIE. (*Easily.*) Oh, I try and keep up. (JUD *looks at him.*) I read that play you wrote a couple of years ago.

JUD. Oh?

SCOTTIE. It was wonderful.

JUD. Thanks, but Mom said you once told Sonja Henie she was a great actress.

SCOTTIE. Well, I thought you both needed encouragement. Anyway, didn't it win some sort of workshop production?

JUD. Yes—but it just confirmed my suspicions that the stage is no longer a valid platform for a serious writer.

SCOTTIE. (*Gently.*) Play was that much of a disaster, huh?

JUD. (*Dryly.*) Well, nobody said anything I could use in the ads.

SCOTTIE. Jud, at the risk of sounding like an elder statesman, don't you think you should go around the track a couple more times before settling for a seat in the grandstand?

JUD. I don't follow you.

SCOTTIE. I was just wondering about this sudden urge to become Mr. Chips.

JUD. Yes, well, let me try to answer that question.

SCOTTIE. It's not a press conference, kid. Relax.

JUD. (*Earnestly.*) I decided that if I got a Ph.D. in History it would give me a number of options. I could teach or possibly use my writing ability to make a contribution as a social historian. I applied to Berkeley and was accepted for this fall. My feeling is that it's the correct move. Then when this summer job came up I just couldn't afford to pass it up.

SCOTTIE. When does the job start?

JUD. Well, they wanted me there right away, but

I managed to put them off for a week so I could visit with you.

SCOTTIE. A week? You're only going to be here a week?

JUD. If it's okay with you.

SCOTTIE. Well, I wish you'd consulted me.

JUD. I would have, but— (*A slight shrug.*) —I knew it wouldn't make much difference to you one way or the other. (SCOTTIE *watches* JUD *as he moves up the stairs and EXITS with his bags. He then turns to* MAGGIE.)

SCOTTIE. Look, I know we kid around a lot, but I'd like to ask you a serious question. Who's his father? The Japanese gardener? I mean, there's not one single thing about the kid that's like me. Level with me— was it the pool man with the tight jeans and the tattoo? (MAGGIE *does not speak.*) How is he?

MAGGIE. He put himself through college with extra jobs, he graduated summa cum laude, he looks out for the other two kids, he's never touched drugs or alcohol and he keeps his room clean.

SCOTTIE. Yeah, he worries me. (*She grins.*) Well, doesn't he worry you? I mean, the kid's twenty years old and he dresses like he's out of a Chekhov play.

MAGGIE. I know he can be tactless and abrasive, Scottie, but it's just his manner.

SCOTTIE. No, it's not that. Despite his total lack of social graces, I find the kid amusing. I just wish he was more amused. Is his face always that clenched?

MAGGIE. Jud's a very serious person. Always has been.

SCOTTIE. Not always. Whenever I used to put on that chicken costume—the one I brought home from the studio—he used to roll around on the floor screaming with laughter.

MAGGIE. Scottie, he was eight years old then.

SCOTTIE. (*Suddenly.*) I want him to stay, Maggie.

MAGGIE. (*Puzzled.*) Scottie, this opportunity is very important to him.

SCOTTIE. Well, it's very important to me that he stays.

MAGGIE. Why?

SCOTTIE. Because I'd like to get to know him! What the hell do you want, Maggie—a couple of choruses of 'Sunrise, Sunset'? I'd like him to know me!

MAGGIE. There's something you're not telling me, Scottie.

SCOTTIE. What makes you say that?

MAGGIE. You could always make me laugh but you could never lie to me.

SCOTTIE. (*Evasively.*) Yeah. I remember when I had the bad taste to show up at the property settlement wearing a tattered tramp suit and carrying a tin cup filled with pencils. You were the only one who had the grace to laugh. Unfortunately, the judge didn't. (*She doesn't smile but keeps her eyes on him.*) I just spent a week in the hospital. Turns out I'm in less than perfect health.

MAGGIE. How imperfect.

SCOTTIE. Well, when they advise you to get your affairs in order you tend to think they've posted the closing notice. Some kind of blood disorder. I guess after all the abuse I've heaped on it—it finally turned on me. I'm sorry, Maggie. I didn't want to burden you with—but— (*He sees her eyes are filled.*) —Hey, take it easy. (*He gives her his handkerchief.*) You know, this is very flattering. Remember 'The Scoundrel' where Noel Coward had to come back to earth until he found someone who would cry for him? I'm sorry, I always did have this insane compulsion to fill any conversational gap.

MAGGIE. There's no possibility of a mistake?

SCOTTIE. No mistake and no cure. Damnedest thing. It was right out of 'Dark Victory'. I mean, I found myself saying all those lines. You know, 'How long have I got, Doc?' I'm not sure but I think I even said, 'Give it to me straight.' I've always said Warner Brothers have a lot to answer for.

MAGGIE. Have you told anyone else yet?

SCOTTIE. No. I thought I might take out an ad in 'Variety.' Nothing too splashy—maybe a half page discreetly edged in black saying, 'Scottie Templeton is going to croak in three months so you'd better damned well be nice to him.' What the hell—once in a lifetime opportunity.

MAGGIE. Scottie, when are you going to stop using the whole world as a straight man? (*He looks at her.*)

SCOTTIE. I've found you can't stay hysterical for three days, Maggie. I mean it's really a case of "No ass to kick and no heart to appeal to." But there is a lighter side. I don't know too many people who could say they've lived exactly the way they've wanted. I found great comfort in that. Well, let's not get carried away—not great—but a comfort neverthe-less. Look, let's get off this unfortunate subject. The only reason I brought it up was because of Jud.

MAGGIE. I can understand why you want him to stay, Scottie.

SCOTTIE. It's not purely selfish. I wasn't kidding when I said he worries me, Maggie. He seems to lack any—I don't know—zest for life—any *joy*. Well, I've been thinking—I can't leave him any money, not even too many childhood memories— (*As she goes to speak.*) —No, it's okay—let me finish.

My first idea was to leave him a list of the two hundred best maitre d's in the country and what to tip them for a good table. After I got that nonsense out of my system, I figured out that the one thing I know how to do well is have fun. If I could teach him that, it's something. Not exactly Tara, but something. Now I don't know how the hell I do that, but I need some time to take a shot at it.

MAGGIE. Why don't you tell him the truth, Scottie?

SCOTTIE. Oh, I can't do that.

MAGGIE. Why not?

SCOTTIE. It'd depress the hell out of him. (*A beat.*) Could you get him to stay?

MAGGIE. I'll talk to him. (*He watches her as she starts to move up the stairs.*)

SCOTTIE. Hey, tell me something. (*She stops, looks at him.*) Why did we ever call it quits?

MAGGIE. Think hard and it'll come back to you.

SCOTTIE. I have and I keep coming up blank.

MAGGIE. You didn't think you had talent and I did.

SCOTTIE. I always found that very touching.

MAGGIE. No, you didn't. You found it annoying. (*She EXITS. He stands looking up after her as the front door opens and* LOU DANIELS, *wearing a raincoat,* BUSTLES IN.)

LOU. I've been trying to reach you all morning. Why is your phone off the hook? (*He replaces the receiver.*)

SCOTTIE. I heard Liz Taylor was in town and I didn't want to be bothered with all those pleading phone calls.

LOU. Well, we have a couple of emergencies. Why didn't you phone me from Vegas?

SCOTTIE. I was on vacation.

LOU. So you couldn't pick up a phone?

SCOTTIE. Will you listen to you? It's like working for Molly Goldberg.

LOU. I got about a million calls, Scottie. (*He pulls out a handful of crumpled envelopes from his pocket.*)

SCOTTIE. Give me the personal ones first. (LOU *sighs, shakes his head, consults his envelopes.*)

LOU. Well, there are the usual number of guys who came into town and phoned to see where the action is. Oh yeah, Doctor Petrelli called twice this morning. Said it was urgent.

SCOTTIE. I'll get back to her.

LOU. Is it something to do with those hot flashes you were having?

SCOTTIE. I was *not* having hot flashes. I just had a couple of dizzy spells.

LOU. Brought on by the incredible carnal demands made nightly upon your tired, old body?

SCOTTIE. She said that?

LOU. No, you did.

SCOTTIE. She's on some public health committee in Washington. I promised I'd help her with the P.R. (MAGGIE *ENTERS, sees* LOU.)

MAGGIE. Lou! (*Comes down stairs and they embrace.*)

LOU. Maggie! Maggie, how are you?

MAGGIE. It's good to see you, Lou.

LOU. Here, let me look at you. (*He steps back to look at her.*) What is it with you? How come you look prettier every time I see you?

MAGGIE. Beats the hell out of me. How are the kids?

LOU. Very active. They help keep me middle-aged.

MAGGIE. Next time I'm in town we'll have to catch up. Right now I'm so far behind schedule. Would you do me a favor and call me a cab? (LOU *starts to phone.*)

SCOTTIE. Why don't you flag one down, it'll be faster?

LOU. Dump that stiff you're with and meet me outside. (*He EXITS. She turns to* SCOTTIE.)

MAGGIE. It's all set.

SCOTTIE. What did you tell him?

MAGGIE. That you haven't seen him for two years, that you'd been looking forward to spending some time together, that you'd made plans and that you wanted him to stay.

SCOTTIE. (*Incredulously.*) And he bought all that?

MAGGIE. He seemed to think it was a reasonable request.

SCOTTIE. I'll be damned.

MAGGIE. Scottie, you are his father. (SCOTTIE *does an "are you sure" take.* MAGGIE, *amused, crosses to pick up her suitcase.*)

SCOTTIE. When does your plane leave?

MAGGIE. Tomorrow morning.. (*A beat.*) Anything I can do—to help? (*He looks at her for a moment.*)

SCOTTIE. Come back and have a drink with me tonight. I'd like to look at your funny face for a while. (*She nods, touches him lightly and EXITS.* JUD *ENTERS carrying his camera and some film, comes down stairs.*) Hey, kid, I'm sorry about screwing up your summer, but I appreciate your spending time with your old man.

JUD. That's okay. I mean I'm very flattered.

SCOTTIE. (*Puzzled.*) Flattered?

JUD. I mean—well, I guess I can find something to do. (*He moves away, sits and loads camera during the following.*)

SCOTTIE. Well, it won't be a total loss. I know a girl who's been crouched in the sprint position waiting for you to get into town. (SCOTTIE *gets his jacket from railing and puts it on.*)

JUD. Why would she want to meet me?

SCOTTIE. I told her you were often mistaken for Joe Namath.

JUD. What am I supposed to do when she sees me?

SCOTTIE. Tell her you had a bad flight.

JUD. Thanks, but at this stage, I'm not interested in quick, casual relationships.

SCOTTIE. Why not? They're the best kind. Look, have I ever steered you wrong before? When you were sixteen, didn't I arrange your first date with that cute ballet dancer from Sadler Wells? (JUD *moves to window, looks thorugh viewfinder.*)

JUD. Well, since you brought it up, when I got back to Canada, I found out she'd given me a dose of V.D.

SCOTTIE. My God, why didn't you tell me?

JUD. The damage was done. I mean, it was too late to do anything to prevent it.

SCOTTIE. Well, maybe for *you.* Look, trust me on this one. She—

JUD. Dad, I like to make my own friends, okay? (*As* SCOTTIE *looks at him.*) Anyway, I want to use the time here to get some work done. (JUD *goes back to fiddling with his camera.* SCOTTIE *watches him for a moment.*)

SCOTTIE. Hey, whatever happened to that girlfriend you had in Pennsylvania?

JUD. (*Puzzled.*) What girl?

SCOTTIE. No, that's not it! You're supposed to say 'Erie?' and then I say, 'Well, I always thought she was a little *weird.*' (JUD *is still looking at him in a puzzled fashion.*) It's an old vaudeville routine we used to do. Don't you remember?

JUD. I had to be six years old then.

SCOTTIE. But we used to do it practically every day. My God, how could you forget it?

JUD. (*Dryly.*) Maybe it's because I always had to play straight man.

SCOTTIE. Kid, you're no trouper. (LOU *RE-ENTERS, stops, looks at* SCOTTIE.)

LOU. You know something? Of all the women you've had I like her the best.

SCOTTIE. (*After a beat—gently.*) Me too, Lou. (*As* JUD *gets to his feet.*) You remember Jud. (*They shake hands.*)

JUD. Nice to see you again, Mr. Daniels.

LOU. You're looking good, kid. All that ice and snow up there must agree with you.

SCOTTIE. It's the whale blubber and reindeer milk, Lou. (*To* JUD.) Lou thinks anything north of the Stage Delicatessen is Caribou Country.

JUD. (*Starting to exit.*) I'll get out of your way.

SCOTTIE. No, stick around—see the pathetic way your old man makes a living. (*He moves to get a tattered, old photo album from the mantel.*) Here—since you're a camera buff—this may amuse you. (*Handing him the album.*) I came across it a couple of days ago when I was cleaning out.

JUD. (*Looking at it—puzzled.*) A family album?

SCOTTIE. That's my old man. Taken overseas during the first World War . . .

LOU. Scottie!

SCOTTIE. Okay. (*To* JUD.) We'll get back to the Templeton Saga later. (JUD *sits on the ottoman and studies the album as* SCOTTIE *sits opposite* LOU.) What's the emergency?

LOU. It's Brad Lucas.

SCOTTIE. (*To* JUD.) Brad Lucas is the host of a 'hard hitting' television interview show who asks opening questions like, 'Okay, you're a whore, you're a pimp. Now how does it feel to be the scum of the earth?' (*To* Lou.) What does he want?

Lou. He wants to tell everyone he's gay.

Scottie. Was there ever any question?

Lou. We're talking about the public. His agent thinks it's a bad career move. He's afraid it'll hurt his ratings. You got any ideas?

Scottie. Couldn't he just say he's bisexual? That way he'd only lose half the country. (*As* Lou *looks at him.*) Okay, okay—I'll talk to him. What else do you have?

Lou. Marvin Schneider.

Scottie. (*To* Jud.) Marvin Schneider produces 'meaningful' situation comedies. Nice chap, but can empty a room faster than any man I know.

Lou. (*Handing him slip.*) He's at the Sherry and wants you to call him.

Scottie. (*To* Jud.) Isn't this fascinating?

Jud. (*Blurting.*) I don't know how you stand it. (*There is a small pause.*)

Scottie. (*Mildly.*) Well, I know it's not brain surgery, son—but it has its moments.

Jud. I'm sorry. I just mean dealing with all these people. You know—actors.

Scottie. Oh, but I like actors. They have a sense of occasion. I mean, if you invite them to a party, they *contribute.* Not like your relatives from Oregon. (*To* Lou.) Lou, I hope that's all because this is Jud's first day in town and we'd like some time to play together.

Jud. It's okay. There's an Ansel Adams exhibition at the Museum of Modern Art I want to see.

Lou. No, there's nothing else pressing. (*Checking envelopes.*) Oh, Audrey's in town and has been trying to reach you.

SCOTTIE. (*To* JUD.) That's Audrey Lawrence. She's a faded, semi-famous tennis player.

JUD. I know who she is. She used to be my stepmother.

SCOTTIE. Just seeing if you were paying attention. (LOU *rises, crosses to door.*) Where you rushing off to Lou?

LOU. I have to get up to Boston to see that show in previews. I'll call you tonight. (LOU *has been looking at* SCOTTIE.) You okay, pal? You're beginning to almost look your age.

SCOTTIE. (*Shrugs.*) You don't go to Vegas for a rest cure.

LOU. Well, it's nice to have you back, kid. (*To* JUD.) Try and get Peter Pan here to slow down, huh? His wires are beginning to show. (*He EXITS.*)

SCOTTIE. Lou is a born father. Even when he was thirteen years old, he wore an overcoat, a hat and a scarf and said and things like 'Life isn't all fun and games, kid.'

JUD. He seems like a nice man.

SCOTTIE. Not to mention the best audience I ever had.

JUD. That's important?

SCOTTIE. Well, nobody likes to go through life playing to an empty theatre. (*He notices the loose photo* JUD *is holding.*) You never knew her, did you? My mother—your grandmother?

JUD. No.

SCOTTIE. British you know. She wasn't a particularly sensual woman—I somehow gathered that her idea of sex was to lie back and think of England. And as we used to say in the soaps—'Why am I telling you all this—a perfect stranger?'

JUD. Well—it did cross my mind.

SCOTTIE. I thought an echo of my past might provide a hint to your future. You're not really going out in public in that coat, are you?

JUD. I don't really think clothes are that important.

SCOTTIE. They're not—but then nothing is. However, we do have to do our best to keep up the pretense, don't we? Our first stop will be my tailor's.

JUD. Dad, this is the last day of the exhibition and I don't want to miss it.

SCOTTIE. Okay. Tell you what—I'll get some work done then come back here and we'll play about two. Now we can either visit my money at the track or if gambling isn't your game, we can go over to a place on Forty-second Street where they let you wrestle a naked lady.

JUD. Please don't feel you have to entertain me.

SCOTTIE. Oh, it wasn't for you. Last time they let me win two falls out of three.

JUD. Look, I appreciate what you're doing, but I don't have time for all that. I mean, I don't see the point.

SCOTTIE. There is no point. It's called 'having a good time.'

JUD. Well, I'd prefer to have a good time my own way, okay? (*He checks watch.*) I'll see you later, huh? (SCOTTIE *nods and turns away.* JUD *moves to the front door.*)

SCOTTIE. (*Suddenly—abruptly.*) I want to spend time with you, Jud! (JUD *turns and looks at* SCOTTIE, *too surprised at his tone to say anything.*) I mean, I'd like to catch up with what you've been doing with your funny little life.

JUD. (*Slightly puzzled.*) Sure. I'll be around. (JUD *EXITS.* SCOTTIE *shakes his head in frustration, moves to phone, notices the note* SALLY *has left, picks it up, makes a decision, and dials.*)

SCOTTIE. (*Into phone.*) Hello, is this the residence of Miss Sally Haines?—Well, this is Doctor Bates who operated on you last week. Uh, I don't quite know how to broach this, Miss Haines, but I seem to have mislaid my left shoe and I was wondering if you've been experiencing a stuffy feeling when you sit down. (*He grins, changes his tone.*) Listen, my love, my son is firmly ensconced. I thought I might rub the two of you together and see if you create any sparks. For the next couple of hours he's at a photographic exhibit at the Museum of Modern Art. One slight problem. Unlike his father, he has this bizarre obsession about not being introduced to attractive young ladies— (*The LIGHTS SLOWLY START TO DIM on the living room and a SPOTLIGHT DOWNSTAGE LEFT and the BULBS surrounding the proscenium SLOWLY COME UP. In the spotlight we see* HILARY, *a blonde, well-groomed, attractive woman with a casual, friendly manner.* SCOTTIE, *continues into phone.*) So, it'll have to be what we used to call a 'meet cute.' You game?— Sally, somewhere along the way a piece of me fell off and became you. (*By now the living room is DARK and the SPOTLIGHT is UP FULL on* HILARY.)

HILARY. Okay, maybe it's about time I introduced myself, but if you think I'm going to tell you my real name, you're crazy. Think of me as Hilary, okay? I've been living in the Bahamas for the past four years and there's only one person who I'd fly back to New York for and that's Scottie Templeton. I used to be in the entertainment business, but my entertaining was done privately—more on a one-to-one basis (*She grins.*) Let's just say I was a girl who made ends meet by making ends meet. We all straight? Okay,

Scottie and I had a relationship. First as a sometime client—then as a friend. Most of the time, he'd drop by just to shoot the breeze and have a few laughs. He knew I'd set myself a time limit and a goal. I wanted to retire from 'show business' and open up a little travel agency. I was right on schedule and doing just fine until six months before my planned retirement when I got busted twice in a row. Then I got sick and between the lawyers and the doctors, I was suddenly knocked right out of the box. Anyway, I'm sitting there contemplating a fate worse than death when Scottie drops by, insists that I get dressed, takes me over to the Hilton Hotel and waltzes me into the banquet room. As I walk in, a hundred guys stand up and applaud. No kidding—a hundred. And they all look familiar. Very familiar. Scottie had rounded up all my clients to give me a Testimonial Dinner. He said I was being forcibly retired. And you should have heard the speeches. I still get misty-eyed thinking about them. They even gave me a gold watch. Better still, he'd charged them two hundred and fifty bucks a plate. (*The SPOTLIGHT on her STARTS TO DIM and the living room is gradually ILLUMI-NATED to reveal* JUD *and* SALLY. JUD *is coming downstairs with a blanket.* SALLY *is sitting on the floor with a shopping bag of food.*) Three days later I was in the Bahamas setting up my own travel agency. So now we're paying tribute to Scottie and do I have to explain why I'm here? I'm here for the same reason you are. I love him. (*THE SPOTLIGHT is out on* HILARY. *The scrim flies out.*)

SALLY. You sure your father won't mind us turning his place into a picnic ground?

JUD. It'll probably make his day.

SALLY. (*Starting to put food on blanket.*) There— this is going to work out just fine.

JUD. Well, a lot better than your original idea. If it had rained we'd have been soaked.

SALLY. Your father must be pretty successful to afford a place like this.

JUD. Not really. (*She looks at him.*) His partner—his boss really—is an old friend of his. He owns the building. (*A somewhat awkward pause.*) I've always liked the name Sally.

SALLY. Yeah? I didn't but I finally came back to it.

JUD. You had other names?

SALLY. Dozens. (*She continues to set out food.*) My father was a construction engineer and we moved around a lot so I was always the new girl in town. (*She takes a bite from a pastrami sandwich.*) I was kind of a shy, scruffy-looking kid so it was tough making friends. (*She holds the sandwich for him as he takes a bite.*) Here, try this pastrami—it's terrific. Anyway, I hit on this dumb idea. I used to take the first name of the most popular girl from the last school. Believe it or not, for about three months, I was actually named Corky.

JUD. I can't imagine you ever being unattractive or shy.

SALLY. Well, I got over it.

JUD. How?

SALLY. (*Matter-of-factly.*) I grew tits.

JUD. (*Deadpan.*) Funny, that didn't work for me. (*She looks at him, notices him staring at her.*)

SALLY. What is it?

JUD. Oh, nothing. I just can't get over your being here.

SALLY. (*Puzzled.*) You invited me.

JUD. I know. It's just— (*Happily—blurting.*) Well, you're my first pick-up! (*She is too surprised to say anything. A slight pause.*) I guess this is a good time to tell you that my nickname is 'El Blurto.' (*Awkwardly.*) I didn't mean to sound offensive. It's just that I've never been very good at—meeting girls and I'm very pleased you're here.

SALLY. (*Amused.*) Yeah, well don't get too carried away. I practically had to tackle you around the knees to stop you leaving the Museum. (*She hands him a bottle of pickles to open.*) Why didn't you talk to me the first time I approached you?

JUD. I didn't know what to say.

SALLY. You have trouble talking to people?

JUD. I got out of practice.

SALLY. You were a monk?

JUD. I used to stutter. When that cleared up I had trouble—getting the hang of it again. (*Awkwardly.*) It's not as strange as it sounds.

SALLY. (*Grinning.*) Wanta bet? (*They smile at one another.*) You see how well this is all working out? You're holding up your end of the conversation beautifully.

JUD. You want to hear something hysterical? Well, interesting maybe. (*He tries to open the bottle without success.*) My father's very—you know—glib. No—socially adept. Very gregarious—you'd like him—everybody does. He's not at all like me. (*He gives up on bottle.*) Anyway, during the winter, I used to carry around this exercise book so I could jot down amusing things to say when I saw him in the summer. I tried it a couple of times but then I gave up.

SALLY. Why?

JUD. A certain look of panic comes into people's eyes when they're confronted by a fourteen-year-old Henny Youngman. (*He turns the jar top the opposite way and it unscrews easily.*) Why'd you want to meet me anyway?

SALLY. Oh, I'm always attracted to eccentrics. (*Sitting back.*) Do you visit your father every summer?

JUD. No, I used to but I haven't seen him for a couple of years.

SALLY. Why not?

JUD. (*Shrugs.*) I had summer jobs—one thing and another—you know.

SALLY. What made you decide to see him this summer?

JUD. (*Evasively.*) Oh, a lot of reasons.

SALLY. You don't like to talk about anything personal, do you?

JUD. (*Half kidding.*) Yeah—well, I don't know you very well. Here— (*He gives her a cushion for her back. She looks at him for a moment.*)

SALLY. Thanks. Can I have a bite of your pickle?

JUD. (*Indicating.*) There's one right here.

SALLY. No, I want a bite of yours.

JUD. (*Offering it.*) Here, have a whole pickle.

SALLY. No, just a bite. (*She takes a fairly large bite.*) There—now we've shared a pickle.

JUD. I noticed that.

SALLY. So now we know each other a lot better and you can tell me anything. (*He looks at her for a moment.*)

JUD. Okay—I wanted to tie up some loose ends. (*She doesn't understand.*) I realized my father and I were both getting older and that this was probably the last chance we'd have to—reach some understanding.

SALLY. See, was that so hard? (*She leans over and kisses him lightly. They gaze at one another.*) You really *hated* me taking a bite of your pickle, didn't you?

JUD. (*Earnestly.*) It was nothing personal. I don't like *anybody* touching my food.

SALLY. (*Teasing.*) And you don't think *that's* weird? (*He looks at her for a moment and then impulsively kisses her. The front door opens and* SCOTTIE *ENTERS. He looks at them and fakes outrage.*)

SCOTTIE. My God, you've got a girl in here again! You'd think after that shabby episode with the chambermaid, you'd have learned your lesson! (*The two grin and get to their feet. To* SALLY.) Hello, I'm Scott Templeton—Jud's teenage father. (*To* JUD.) My, wherever did you find *her?*

JUD. (*Proudly.*) This is Sally Haines, Dad, and I found her at the Museum of Modern Art.

SCOTTIE. (*Puzzled.*) I didn't think they let you bring the exhibits home.

SALLY. Would you like to join our picnic? We have lots of food.

SCOTTIE. Only on one condition. There'll be absolutely no hugging and kissing.

JUD. Well, we'll try to control ourselves if you will. (*SCOTTIE looks at* JUD *in surprise, breaks into a delighted grin, looks at* SALLY.)

SCOTTIE. My God, he made a joke! You must be good for him.

SALLY. (*Gesturing.*) Well, shall we dine?

SCOTTIE. You go ahead. I think I'll make myself a drink first.

SALLY. You sit down. I'll do it.

SCOTTIE. The bar's behind the— (*She is already on her way to the bar.*)

SALLY. I know, I know—press the secret button. (*She presses the button and the bar revolves around.*

We see JUD's *reaction.*) What'll you have? I used to be a cocktail waitress at Lake Tahoe so— (*She stops talking, her back still to them, as the realization hits her. Quietly:*) Oh—no. (*She turns and looks at* JUD *who stares first at her and then looks at* SCOTTIE.)

SCOTTIE. (*Quietly.*) Oh, yes. (*He turns to* JUD *who is hurt and angry but is trying to cover it.*) Listen, son, I think I can explain—

JUD. Oh, come on, Dad—I knew it was a setup all along.

SALLY. (*Surprised.*) You did? How?

JUD. I checked in the mirror this morning and I'm not Robert Redford. (*They are both looking at him. He attempts a laugh.*) Hey, who do you think you're dealing with here? I happen to be a college graduate.

SALLY. But if you knew from the start, why did you go along with it?

JUD. Listen, I never said my father didn't have *taste.* I mean, I'm no dope. (JUD *turns away to the picnic.*)

SALLY. I'm really sorry, Jud.

JUD. There's nothing to be sorry about. Listen, are we going to eat or what? (*She turns to* SCOTTIE, *shrugs.*)

SALLY. I guess I overplayed my role, Scottie.

SCOTTIE. There's no harm done, my love. It seems you got the part anyway. (*He checks wristwatch.*) You know, maybe I should take a small raincheck on dinner. I do have a late date and I have to perfume my body and slip into something stunning. (*Moving up stairs. He stops halfway up stairs, turns.*) Sally, don't be put off by the kid's impression of the Reverend Davidson. Underneath that grim exterior, there beats the heart of a sex maniac. At least I hope so— for his sake.

JUD. (*With a slight edge.*) Yes—well, if I ever need a reference I'll certainly know where to go.

SCOTTIE. (*Evenly.*) Sorry, son. There'll be no more cheering from the cheap seats. (*He EXITS.*)

SALLY. That's just about the most charming man I've ever met.

JUD. Built a whole career on it. Never met a man he couldn't charm.

SALLY. He just wanted you to have a good time, Jud. Is that any reason for putting him down?

JUD. (*Hotly.*) That has nothing to do with it! I told you I knew from the beginning he'd set it up.

SALLY. Oh come off it! You may have fooled Scottie, but I was there, remember? Anyway, what did he do that was so terrible?

JUD. My father's made a living from being a court jester and a glorified pimp. Well, I don't like him pimping for me, okay? (*She looks at him for a moment.*)

SALLY. If he's a pimp, what does that make me?

JUD. (*Turning away.*) I don't make those sort of judgments.

SALLY. You don't make judgments! That's all you do!

JUD. How could you possibly know what I do or don't do?

SALLY. I spent the afternoon with you. You see things in black and white. You label people. Well people aren't things they're human. They make mistakes—like your father.

JUD. Look, you don't know a damn thing about him!

SALLY. No, but whatever he is, I'm sure having a tight-assed son like you hasn't helped much. (*She moves towards door, turns.*) If you're so jealous of your father, why do you stay with him?

JUD. Jealous of him? Jealous of *what?*

SALLY. You're the one who likes to play God. You figure it out. (*She EXITS. JUD, angry and frustrated, starts to clean up, gives up, sits, The DOORBELL rings. JUD opens the front door. SCOTTIE, dressed in a ridiculous-looking chicken costume, rushes into the room, moving in an odd bird-like gait, crosses DOWNSTAGE CENTER, struts across the stage then back up, rushing toward JUD who is staring, speechless by the front door. JUD jumps out of the way as the CHICKEN rushes by, settles between the table and couch and lays a large football-sized white egg. Proudly the CHICKEN bows and then collapses on its back on the floor, exhausted. When the egg is laid JUD breaks down into hysterical laughter. He picks up the egg and sets it on the table and sits beside it. SCOTTIE removes the chicken head.*)

SCOTTIE. (*Finally—in his own voice.*) Well, it's good to see you can still laugh.

JUD. (*Wiping his eyes.*) It's stupid—it's not funny —it's so corny!

SCOTTIE. What do you expect at these prices—Noel Coward? (SCOTTIE *flops on sofa.*)

JUD. I didn't expect anything.

SCOTTIE. Well, I knew you were upset and I thought it might be easier to apologize if I got you laughing first.

JUD. How'd you get around to the front door?

SCOTTIE. The backstairs. (*Sitting up.*) Where's Sally?

JUD. She left.

SCOTTIE. Why?

JUD. I think I called her a whore. (SCOTTIE *looks at him for a moment.*)

SCOTTIE. Well now, as Lana Turner said when she saw Judith Evelyn, 'Of course, I would have played it differently.' Why did you do that?

JUD. I guess I overreacted to the whole—situation.

SCOTTIE. Well, you've certainly caught my interest.

JUD. It's complicated. This afternoon, when I met Sally, I guess I wanted to—well, show her off. I mean, you were never around to see me hit a home run in Little League. Not that I actually ever hit a home run—but if I had—well— (JUD *moves to clean up the remains of the picnic and puts them on the hearth along with the blanket.*) Anyway, I thought my scoring with a girl would be more meaningful to you. That's why I phoned you to come home and meet her.

SCOTTIE. (*Gently.*) It was that important to you?

JUD. I've never been very successful with women. I seem to lack—polish.

SCOTTIE. Of course you do. You're still a rough draft. (SCOTTIE *crosses up to the piano to take off the chicken costume.*)

JUD. You look ridiculous.

SCOTTIE. Bring back memories?

JUD. How come you kept it all these years?

SCOTTIE. Sentimental reasons. (SCOTTIE *finishes taking off the chicken costume.*)

JUD. When you split with Mom—why didn't you tell me about it?

SCOTTIE. You're going back a few years, aren't you?

JUD. It's okay—I didn't really expect an answer.

SCOTTIE. Was it that hard for you?

JUD. I got used to it. It's just that—I got up one morning and you'd gone.

SCOTTIE. I couldn't explain it to myself. You were very young—I didn't know the right words.

JUD. What about afterwards?

SCOTTIE. Afterwards I didn't have the guts. I'm sorry. (*There is a pause.*)

JUD. Yes—well, I appreciate the directness of your answer. (*Holds up wine.*) You want some wine?

SCOTTIE. No, and I'm not going to stand around and watch you become a hopeless alcoholic over a lovers' tiff.

JUD. She's just a girl I've known for about six hours, Dad. (SCOTTIE *looks at him for a moment.*)

SCOTTIE. You're very wise, son. You seem to have developed the ability to project—to stand back and pragmatically see a situation for what it is and where it'll lead.

JUD. Is that so bad?

SCOTTIE. No—but sometimese I wonder if you deprive yourself of—well, the experience. I guess the trouble with being sensitive and all-knowing is that you never have the luxury of going off half-cocked and making a total ass of yourself. Sorry, I didn't intend to lapse into social work, but I suspect you'd like to see her again.

JUD. How do I do that?

SCOTTIE. Well, it's been my experience that the best course of action in this sort of situation is begging and pleading.

JUD. You think I should grovel?

SCOTTIE. Grovelling's good. Get down on your knees and kiss the hem of her dress if you have to.

JUD. Okay, if grovelling's what it takes, I'll grovel.

SCOTTIE. Good. It'll make a man out of you. (JUD *moves to get his coat as* SCOTTIE *crosses to the bar and pours a brandy.*)

JUD. What are you going to do?

SCOTTIE. I suppose I can find some work to do. There's always someone who wants to get their picture

in the paper. (SCOTTIE *sits and plays his 'Unfinished'*
on the piano.)

JUD. You know, a couple of years ago I came across
some of the short stories you wrote before you went to
the Coast. (SCOTTIE *stops playing.*)

SCOTTIE. You never told me that.

JUD. They were very good.

SCOTTIE. Not really.

JUD. I thought so.

SCOTTIE. Well, they fooled a lot of people. Story of
my life. All the form and none of the ability.

JUD. Why did you stop writing? Didn't you feel you
had anything to say?

SCOTTIE. And I didn't even say it very well.

JUD. It was that simple?

SCOTTIE. You really want the long answer? (JUD *sits*
on steps. SCOTTIE *leans against the railing.*) Okay,
when I was about seven—now aren't you sorry you
asked?—my father took me to see a Christmas panto-
mime show. He knew the stage manager and afterwards we went backstage. Well, if the show was magic
—this was heaven. I mean, you'd have to be crazy to
choose reality over this. I suppose I used my writing
as a ticket to the show. Are we nodding off yet?

JUD. No. I was just thinking it doesn't explain the
quality of the work I read.

SCOTTIE. Oh, I'm not saying I was totally without
talent. I was a pretty good literary mimic. Good
enough to get me to the West Coast, anyway.

JUD. And you stopped writing?

SCOTTIE. Not immediately. When I went to Hollywood, I discovered it was phony, tacky, superficial
and vulgar—everything I'd ever wanted. With all these
distractions, my concentration—never my strong suit
anyway—dwindled to that of a monkey. The obvious

solution was to become a producer. The rest, as they say, is showbiz history.

JUD. It doesn't bother you that you have nothing you can point to with any pride?

SCOTTIE. Well, I'd always rather hoped it would be you. (JUD *reddens, gets up, stands awkwardly for a moment.*)

JUD. (*Formally.*) Yes—well, I've enjoyed having this talk.

SCOTTIE. So have I, Mr. Carstairs, and I'll certainly talk to the little woman about that insurance policy.

JUD. I'm sorry. Sometimes—when something affects me emotionally I make inappropriate responses.

SCOTTIE. So do I, son. So do I. (*The moment is broken by the front DOORBELL. JUD opens it to reveal a very angry DR. GLADYS PETRELLI.*)

GLADYS. What the hell do you think you're doing?

SCOTTIE. Whatever happened to 'hello'? This is my son, Jud. Jud, this is an old family retainer, Doctor Gladys Petrelli, who happens to be crazy about my body.

JUD. How do you do? (GLADYS *manages a curt nod.*)

SCOTTIE. Jud's off on a romantic mission and I was giving him the benefit of my vast experience in that area.

GLADYS. This isn't a social call, Scottie.

SCOTTIE. Sure, that's what you always say. Look, I've told you a million times, Gladys, I will *not* take my clothes off unless there's a nurse present. (*To* JUD.) And as for you—I don't want to have to sit up worrying about you so I want you home— (*Checking watch.*) on the dot of Thursday.

JUD. I'll do my best. Nice meeting you, Doctor. (JUD *EXITS.*)

SCOTTIE. You know, for an eminent physician, your bedside manner leaves a lot to be desired.

GLADYS. Don't play games with me, Scottie. I left messages for you all day. Why didn't you return my calls?

SCOTTIE. (*Crossing to table LEFT.*) Why are you limping?

GLADYS. (*Following after* SCOTTIE.) Because my feet swell when I fly. I had to leave that conference in Washington and fly back just to see you!

SCOTTIE. Terrific. All the doctors in the country and I had to get the *one* who makes house calls.

GLADYS. Why did you sneak out of the hospital?

SCOTTIE. Because I hated my room and the service was lousy.

GLADYS. Scottie, don't you think it's about time you started acting like a responsible adult?

SCOTTIE. Oh well—if you're going to make impossible demands—

GLADYS. (*All business.*) Didn't you understand what Hal Shumway and I told you the other day? Didn't we spell out why you had to start treatments immediately? Didn't we lay everything on the line?

SCOTTIE. Not everything. I did some reading and there are some charming little side effects you didn't mention like your hair falling out.

GLADYS. So *what?*

SCOTTIE. You *know* how I hate not looking my best. (*She doesn't answer but just moves to the phone and starts to dial.*) What are you doing?

GLADYS. Getting you another room at the hospital.

SCOTTIE. Put the phone down, Gladys. (*She continues to dial.*) Will you put the phone down? (*She ignores him.*) Gladys, do I have to wrestle you to the ground? I have something to say. (*He cuts off her call. She reluctantly hangs up.*)

GLADYS. You've got two minutes, Scottie. (*She sits on the sofa.*)

SCOTTIE. Jud just got into town today and I didn't think I could be too amusing in a hospital bed with a hose stuck up my nose. (*She starts to speak.*) Please, let me finish. (*He sits on the coffee table and massages her foot.*) Let's face it, as a father I've always been strictly a lounge act. I needed some time to clean up my image.

GLADYS. Stop tap dancing, Scottie. You've got to go back into that hospital so why not tonight?

SCOTTIE. I'm sorry. I'm afraid my dance card's all filled tonight. (*Looking at her shoe.*) Now, we don't have this in your size, but I think you might like the blue suede sling-back pumps. (*She slips on shoe.*)

GLADYS. All right, not tonight, tomorrow. (SCOTTIE *makes no answer.*) I'll call for you at nine in the morning. Have your bag packed. (*She crosses to pick up her briefcase.*)

SCOTTIE. Were you ever in the Marines?

GLADYS. You need anything to help you sleep?

SCOTTIE. No. Gladys, after these treatments—a fairly normal life?

GLADYS. It won't be all velvet, Scottie, but, with luck, the good times will outweigh the bad.

SCOTTIE. How about sex?

GLADYS. (*Shrugs.*) If you feel like it.

SCOTTIE. At last! Come back here, take your clothes off and lie down on the couch.

GLADYS. Don't make any rash promises.

SCOTTIE. At least give me a kiss—right here. (*He indicates his cheek.*)

GLADYS. I let you feel my foot—that should be enough for you.

SCOTTIE. Gladys, I know we kid around a lot, but I want you to know I'm terrified. (GLADYS *stops, closes door and comes back into room.*)

GLADYS. That's the first normal reaction you've had tonight. You were beginning to worry me.

SCOTTIE. Well, you can't blame me. That orderly has hands like blocks of ice. (*She doesn't smile.*)

GLADYS. How long have we known each other, Scottie?

SCOTTIE. Eight years, but we didn't become intimate until after the hemorrhoid operation.

GLADYS. I remember when you came out of the anesthetic, you demanded to see the baby. You said for that much pain you should have something to show for it. Since that moment, you've been my favorite patient. So you've already got the job. Stop auditioning and let *me* knock myself out for a change. (*A beat.*) See you in the morning. (*She EXITS.* SCOTTIE *sits.*)

SCOTTIE. (*Into phone.*) Hello, operator— Hi there, how are you?— Yes, I think you can, love. I'd like to call a Mr. Lou Daniels at the Ritz Carleton Hotel in Boston, but I seem to have mislaid the number— well, I'd appreciate that. (*During above* SCOTTIE *crosses to bar, pours brandy, lights cigarette while he waits. Disappointed.*) He isn't— Message?— Just tell him his lawyer phoned about the morals charge— That's right— Oh, what the hell, why keep him in suspense? Tell him one of the triplets has dropped charges, but the other two are sticking to their story— He has my number. (*He hangs up, takes a sip of brandy, puts brandy on the bar. After a moment, he tosses his lighted cigarette into the glass of brandy, puts his two fingers in his ears as if waiting for an explosion. He takes his fingers out, stares bleakly ahead.*) Well, I think I've finally gone right 'round the bend. I'm doing bits and nobody's here to see them. And what's worse I'm talking to myself about it. (*He returns the phone to its shelf as the DOORBELL rings.*) Oh, my God—it's the old lady! Estelle, get down from the chandelier! Everyone back into their clothes. Let go of my leg you silly mad goose. I'm coming—I'm coming. (*As he crosses to the front door he undoes his belt so that his pants drop around his ankles. He opens the door to reveal* MAGGIE.) Come in Madam. (*He waddles to piano, peers under.*) It's no good, Gertrude—out from under the piano—the jig is up. Everybody act normal! (*He strikes a pose in the bow of the piano.*)

MAGGIE. (*Stepping into the room.*) Pull your pants up, Scottie.

SCOTTIE. Why? You always said my right leg was my best feature.

MAGGIE. It's still adorable, but I'm a married woman.

SCOTTIE. (*Pulling pants up.*) You always were a loyal little beast.

MAGGIE. Sorry, you had your chance. How are you?

SCOTTIE. (*Shrugs.*) It's been a funny day. (*He closes the door and pulls up pants.*)

MAGGIE. Funny peculiar or funny ha-ha?

SCOTTIE. Funny, I didn't know it was going to turn out this way. Scotch, soda, no ice? (*She nods. He moves to make drink.*)

MAGGIE. How come you remember what everyone drinks? (*She sits on the piano bench.*)

SCOTTIE. I have the soul of a hundred-dollar hooker.

MAGGIE. Did you ever tell you how I knew when you were cheating on me?

SCOTTIE. Well, I wasn't exactly Howard Hughes when it came to covering my tracks.

MAGGIE. You always switched your drink to the one the woman drank.

SCOTTIE. I never did have a strong sense of identity.

MAGGIE. I've been thinking about us all day.

SCOTTIE. So have I. (*He hands her her glass and squirts soda from syphon.*) Listen, this isn't much but— (*Presenting her with syphon.*) —a bunch of the crew chipped in to buy it as a small token of our appreciation.

MAGGIE. Things getting to you, Scottie? (*He looks at her.*) You always get your most manic when you're depressed.

SCOTTIE. I was alone for three whole minutes before you came. You know how I hate that.

MAGGIE. When do you expect Jud?

SCOTTIE. In about two weeks—if he has any sense.

MAGGIE. He's with a girl?

SCOTTIE. She's exactly what he needs, Maggie. I mean, I think she can introduce him to the finer things in life.

MAGGIE. Like what?

SCOTTIE. Laughs, sex, ulcers, alimony—you know, all the good things that make you want to get up in the morning.

MAGGIE. Apart from the sex education course—how are you two getting along?

SCOTTIE. Well, we're not exactly Andy and Judge Hardy yet, but we had a good talk earlier and he started to open up. There's still a lot a scar tissue there, but I have high hopes for us.

MAGGIE. So have I. It'll just take time. (*She realizes what she has said.*) I'm sorry.

SCOTTIE. Don't be. (SCOTTIE *starts to take a drink from his brandy glass but sees the cigarette floating in it. He remembers how it got there—turns to* MAGGIE *to explain but then thinks better of it. He gets up and goes to bar for a fresh drink.)*

MAGGIE. Scottie, do you mind talking about it?

SCOTTIE. My delicate condition? My God, I stop strangers on the street.

MAGGIE. Because if you don't—I don't. I just mean if it helps at all—well, I'm here.

SCOTTIE. Oh, Maggie, Maggie.

MAGGIE. I mean it.

SCOTTIE. Well, it's funny, you don't think about it all the time. At least I don't. I suppose the body has some built-in mechanism. The night they hit me with the news I went through the inevitable 'why me?' stage. I mean, I know some guys who wouldn't be too upset about cashing it all in, but I like it here. Always have. The weird part is that I didn't resent dying. What really bothered me was knowing when. I don't know—somehow it robs the whole event of spontaneity. *(By now he has his drink and is standing on the platform above the couch where* MAGGIE *is still sitting.)* I wished that I could drink more or get religion, but too much liquor makes me sick and somehow God never caught my attention. Eventually, 'why not me?' I accepted it. At this point I somehow expected some incredible revelation—but— *(He shrugs, gives a little laugh.)* —It reminds me of the time I went to see a Pinter play. Half-way through, I turned to a silver-haired old lady who was sitting next to me and said, 'Do you understand any of this?' She patted my hand and said, 'Don't worry, my dear—all will be revealed in the last act.' At the final curtain, I looked at her and she slowly shook her head and said, 'Well, I'm none the wiser.'

But don't worry, if I get any sudden revelations, you'll be the first to know. I'm sorry my love, I didn't mean to turn this into 'An Evening With—' (*There is a pause. Finally.*) I suppose the worst part is the loss. I mean, when a friend dies, you—well, you lose a friend. But when you die, you lose all your friends. (*He raises his glass, dryly.*) Happy days.

MAGGIE. Scottie, I have to leave tomorrow morning, but if you want me to come down later, I will. If you need me.

SCOTTIE. That's okay—it's really not all that imminent. I mean, I'm going to be around for a while. Listen, not to change the subject, but did I ever tell you about the time right after the divorce I took Jud fishing? It was one of those fish farms where you're guaranteed to catch something. Ten bucks a pop. Well, he seemed perfectly happy casting his little rod, so I snuck off to a gin game. When— (*Without his facial expression changing, tears start to stream down his face. He crosses and sits at the table LEFT.*) —I got back, he was standing on a pile of thirty-seven trout. Cost me three hundred and— (*He stops—with an incredulous expression.*) —You know, this is very embarrassing—I've made myself cry. Well, you did—I can't stand kindness. Jesus, I can't believe it, there's a flood of water coming out of my nose. Is my mascara running? I don't understand this. I mean, you of all people know how I hate scenes. My God, you don't think I'm pregnant too, do you? (*He sits, tries to wipe eyes, looks up.*) Listen, let me ask you a question— you don't think I'm being too macho about all this, do you? (MAGGIE *crosses to comfort* SCOTTIE. *She strokes his head, cradles it in her arms and finally kisses him lightly first on the forehead and then on the mouth. They break momentarily and then* SCOTTIE *pulls her down and kisses her again on the mouth. Finally he rises and they move into a passionate em-*

brace.) Times have changed. I used to laugh you into bed. (*The LIGHTS start to dim as they embrace again and the Tribute SPOTLIGHT picks up* Lou *in the DOWNSTAGE RIGHT area.*)

Lou. —And I know some people thought his refusing to take anything seriously held him back in his career. Of course, his friends thought it was his greatest charm. Anyway, he'd been out of work for over a year and an old gambling buddy thought he was finally ready to accept some responsibility. So he hired him to produce this new television series. After a screening of the pilot film for the network an argument developed about which direction the series should take. All through the yelling and shouting, Scottie didn't say a word. Finally, after about twenty minutes, he stood up, held up his hands for silence and said, in a very firm voice, 'Okay, I've been sitting here patiently listening to you all disagree about how we do this series and I think it's about time I said something. It's simply this. I'm the producer of the show, I'm the one who's ultimately responsible, and I want you to know one thing—I'll go either way.' (*LIGHTS start to come up behind the scrim. We see* Maggie *stretched out on the sofa dressed in* Scottie's *robe.* Scottie *is at the bar making fresh drinks.*) Well, he got his laugh, but three days later he was out of a job and he never worked in Hollywood again.

Scottie. (*A la Noel Coward.*) Happy, darling? (*She grins and falls into an old private routine.*)

Maggie. Very happy, and terribly, terribly proud. (*They toast.*)

Scottie. Maggie, I hope you didn't think I took— unfair advantage of the situation. (*She turns to look at him.*) I mean, I don't want you to think it was like the war when I told all those girls I was being shipped to Gaum the next day.

MAGGIE. (*Gently.*) Scottie, shut up.

SCOTTIE. You think I talk too much?

MAGGIE. I've been meaning to tell you. (*They smile at one another.*)

SCOTTIE. Did you know that you're the perfect ex-wife?

MAGGIE. (*Lightly.*) I wouldn't want that to get around.

SCOTTIE. I mean it. No recriminations, no ugly scenes, no hitting. Where did we go wrong?

MAGGIE. Your rear-view mirror's a little rose tinted, Scottie.

SCOTTIE. I don't remember you ever yelling at me.

MAGGIE. I could never *find* you. You should have been around when your child support cheques bounced.

SCOTTIE. Well, it never occurred to me you'd try to *cash* them.

MAGGIE. I could have killed you. Especially after I heard the amusing way you'd ended your career as a producer.

SCOTTIE. Most expensive cheap laugh I ever got. How'd you know about that?

MAGGIE. Jud read it in the 'Hollywood Reporter.'

SCOTTIE. He was *not* amused?

MAGGIE. No . . . He seemed to think his mother was cut out for better things than being a hostess in a pancake house. (*Dryly.*) Frankly, so did I.

SCOTTIE. Do you know what I always liked best about you?

MAGGIE. I could never hold a grudge. I have to go, Scottie.

SCOTTIE. Yes. Well, my love, in case it slips my mind before you leave, I want to thank you.

MAGGIE. For what?

SCOTTIE. Making a man of me, making me feel alive again, giving me a damn good time. Pick any one of the above. (*She starts to the stairs.*) Maggie? (*She turns.*) Why were you so—generous?

MAGGIE. Generous?

SCOTTIE. Forgive me, but naturally it did cross my mind for a moment that I was the grateful recipient of a mercy hump. But Maggie, it was too special for that, wasn't it?

MAGGIE. (*Finally.*) I think there are—areas of our relationship that are best left unexamined, Scottie.

SCOTTIE. Is it still that painful for you?

MAGGIE. (*Gently.*) We blew it.

SCOTTIE. No, I can't even let you take the co-credit for that, my love.

MAGGIE. I was a very old-fashioned girl who wanted all the conventions of marriage. You didn't.

SCOTTIE. Part of me did. Still does. (*A beat.*) I'm sorry.

MAGGIE. So am I. I tried to turn you into something you're not. (*She grins wryly.*) I have to admit, though —you put up a hell of a fight. (*She EXITS. The front door opens,* JUD *ENTERS, stops in some surprise.*)

JUD. Why are you sitting with all the lights out? (*He flicks the LIGHTS on.*)

SCOTTIE. How come you're home so early?

JUD. Sally kicked me out.

SCOTTIE. You struck out?

JUD. (*Grins.*) It's okay, it wasn't your fault, coach. Small problem of a recent appendectomy. Anyway, she thought it would be a nice idea if I spent some time with you.

MAGGIE. (*OFFSTAGE.*) Scottie, I can't find my skirt. (*Wearing a blouse and slip, she comes onto landing and starts down stairs.*) I can't remember if you ripped it off in the heat of passion down there or— (*Halfway down the stairs, she sees* JUD, *stops. Absolutely stunned he looks from one to the other.*)

SCOTTIE. (*Finally.*) Well now, I suppose if you were a private detective, we'd all end up in those funny, grainy black and white photos. (*Seeing* JUD's *expression, he adopts a different tone.*) It was my fault. We started reminiscing and I'm afraid we got a little carried away . . . (*Moving toward* JUD.)

JUD. (*Exploding.*) Get the hell away from me!!

MAGGIE. Jud, you don't understand the situation.

JUD. (*Incredulously.*) Don't understand the situation? I've *always* understood the situation! I have a-a totally amoral—irresponsible, selfish child for a father who doesn't c-c-care who he hurts as long as he gets his own way!

SCOTTIE. (*Quietly.*) Jud, I think we could handle this if—

JUD. How? How are you going to handle it? Are you going to climb into your *chicken costume?!* (SCOTTIE *doesn't say anything.*) My God, how—how do you live with yourself? What reason do you give yourself for getting up in the mornings? I mean, what are you do-d-*doing* here besides taking up space? (SCOTTIE *remains silent.*) Goddamnit, I want some answers! (SCOTTIE *turns away.*) Nothing to say? Well, just tell me one thing—'Dad.' How does it feel to-to— (*Close to angry tears.*) —cheapen everything you touch? (*He pushes past his mother and moves up the stairs.*)

MAGGIE. Jud, you come back down here!

SCOTTIE. Let him go. (*He speaks in a tired, dead voice.*) I'm the one who's going to die, not him. And— I don't give a damn anymore. (*He crosses to the front door, takes his raincoat and EXITS.* JUD, *carrying his camera bag and his duffel bag comes down the stairs and starts toward the door.*)

JUD. I'll let him know where to send the rest of my things.

MAGGIE. (*Without turning.*) Jud, I have to talk to you.

JUD. Well, I don't have to talk to you. (*He looks at her, unbelieving.*) I thought you hated him.

MAGGIE. Oh, grow up!

JUD. I was grown up when I was eight years old!!

MAGGIE. Jud, you can't leave him.

JUD. (*As he grabs coat.*) Why not?

MAGGIE. Because he's dying.

JUD. What?

MAGGIE. He found out a couple of days ago. That's why you can't leave him now. (JUD *stands for a long moment, his face expressionless, then he drops his stuff, and sits facing out front on the steps STAGE RIGHT.*)

JUD. (*Finally.*) Well, I wish I could feel something. But it doesn't really change anything, does it? He's still the same man he's always been.

MAGGIE. He's still your father. (*After a moment, he gets up, picks up his bags.*) Jud, you'll stay?

JUD. I owe it to myself. I'm going to stick around to see if there's anything about the son-of-a-bitch I can admire. (*He moves slowly up the stairs as . . .*)

THE CURTAIN FALLS.

END OF ACT ONE

ACT TWO

Scene 1

The Time—*The present.*

The Scene—*A New York theatre.*

At Rise—*Multiple rows of light bulbs on the proscenium go on and a SPOTLIGHT illuminates Lou in the area DOWNSTAGE RIGHT.*

Lou. Welcome back. Watching Scottie was the best spectator sport I know. Did you know he once ran away with the circus? He was forty-three at the time. After he left L.A. he got a job as a blackjack dealer in Reno. Well, that was like putting Willie Sutton in charge of a Brinks truck. Then he married Audre and spent the next couple of years hanging around damp green locker rooms entertaining lady jocks. He said it was like living in a Ben Gay factory. That's when he took a job with the circus as an advance publicity man. He got to New York flat broke, worked as a tour guide, a rehearsal pianist, a hotel clerk and a salesman at Saks before he came to work with me. He had many jobs but his real talent was for friendship. He kept his old friends and made new ones every day. This next young lady is one of his newest. Her name's Sally Haines. Sally? (*The SPOTLIGHT CROSS FADES to pick up SALLY in the area DOWNSTAGE LEFT.*)

Sally. Hi! Whenever I think of Scottie—I smile. Not long ago, we were out window shopping with

Brandy, my little Yorkie dog. Well, it started to rain and we couldn't get a cab so we decided to take a bus. When we tried to get on the driver stopped us and said dogs weren't allowed on the bus. It was crazy. I mean, Brandy's about— (*She indicates a tiny dog.*) —this big. Anyway, for once in his life, Scottie's charm failed him and we ended up back on the street. By the time the next bus arrived Scottie had acquired a white cane, and put on dark glasses. With Brandy on a leash he tapped his way up the bus steps. Same story. The driver said: 'I'm sorry, sir, dogs aren't allowed.' Scottie said: 'But he's my seeing-eye dog.' The driver stared at tiny little Brandy and said: 'I thought all seeing-eye dogs were German shepherds.' Scottie said: 'You mean he *isn't?*' (*The spot on* SALLY *goes out as the lights come up behind the scrim revealing* MAGGIE *asleep on the couch covered with a blanket. There is a tray with a coffee thermos and two cups on the table LEFT. After a pause the door opens and* SCOTTIE *ENTERS. It is early A.M. He sees* MAGGIE *then crosses to open the closed drapes. The room is suddenly flooded with sunlight.*)

MAGGIE. Fine time to get home. (SCOTTIE *doesn't turn.*)

SCOTTIE. Sophia, you really must stop sneaking into my apartment.

MAGGIE. I was worried about you. (*He turns to look at her.*)

SCOTTIE. What did you think I'd do? (*She shrugs.*) Well, to tell the truth, it did cross my mind to throw myself in front of a cab. But then it seemed rather a tacky thing to do to the driver—so I decided to pin a generous tip to my coat lapel. But working out what twenty percent of my life is somehow slowed my momentum. I mean, what the hell do you tip for a suicide?

MAGGIE. Five thousand dollars.

SCOTTIE. That much?

MAGGIE. Well, you've gone through your life over-tipping—why change now? So what did you do?

SCOTTIE. Well, after realizing that I'd been miscast as Norman Main, I tramped the streets examining my whole life.

MAGGIE. For how long?

SCOTTIE. Five minutes. It's a short subject at best.

MAGGIE. Just didn't hold your interest, huh?

SCOTTIE. You know what jolted me out of it? I'd stopped at an intersection on Fifth when I noticed this marvelous-looking, melancholic, Byronic figure stand-ing on the wet pavement wreathed in steam rising from the gratings. He looked incredibly romantic and forlorn and—I don't know, maybe it was the mood I was in—but the scene touched a chord in me. I stood drinking him in for a few moments before I sensed something familiar about him.

MAGGIE. It was you?

SCOTTIE. My reflection! And don't think I wasn't im-pressed. I tell you Maggie, I looked like an album cover. Then as I stepped forward with a lump in my throat to take a closer look at the reflection, I slipped on some wet garbage and did a pratfall into the gutter. Shows you what happens when you start taking your-self too seriously.

MAGGIE. Sure, that's always been your problem. So what did you do?

SCOTTIE. Went to my club. Everyone was either asleep or dead so I tracked down an all-night gin game.

MAGGIE. Jud's still here.

SCOTTIE. That kid doesn't know a good exit speech when he makes one. Did you tell him I was going to croak?

MAGGIE. I wish you'd stop talking like Humphrey Bogart.

SCOTTIE. Did you?

MAGGIE. No. I felt that should be your decision.

SCOTTIE. Then what made him stay?

MAGGIE. He calmed down. Look, naturally he was upset and—

SCOTTIE. (*Flatly.*) Everything he said was true, Maggie. You don't have to apologize for him.

MAGGIE. You don't have to apologize either.

SCOTTIE. Oh, I'm not. (*He moves away and sits.*) As Polly Adler once said, 'Nothing needs less justification than pleasure.'

MAGGIE. I believe it was Bernard Shaw.

SCOTTIE. It was? You can't trust anyone anymore. Polly told me it was original.

MAGGIE. You'll let him stay? (SCOTTIE *thinks for a moment.*)

SCOTTIE. I had an aunt who used to say, 'Children should be like waffles. You should be able to throw the first one out.'

MAGGIE. Yes, well Jud may be a little charred around the edges, but he's the only child you have. Anyway, whatever happened to your plan to introduce him to the finer things of life?

SCOTTIE. Maybe I was too ambitious. I don't think he has the talent for it.

MAGGIE. He didn't really mean everything he said, Scottie.

SCOTTIE. (*Shrugs.*) Nothing he said came as any surprise.

MAGGIE. Oh?

SCOTTIE. I've always known what I am. The trick has always been to know what I should be. (*She looks at him for a moment, then moves to get her coat.*)

MAGGIE. Scottie, you still living one step ahead of the bailiffs?

SCOTTIE. You don't have to be coy with me, Maggie. If you need cab fare, just ask for it.

MAGGIE. I mean this—situation could be expensive.

SCOTTIE. I'm okay, kid. Matter of fact, I came out two thousand ahead in the gin game. Why are you stalling?

MAGGIE. I don't know how to say goodbye.

SCOTTIE. Well, I'm very good at that. Just give me a very tender, chaste kiss right here . . . (*Pointing to his cheek. She moves to him, kisses him on the cheek, is surprised he doesn't turn his head at the last moment.*)

MAGGIE. I think I'm offended. You never used to let a girl kiss you on the cheek.

SCOTTIE. Lately my timing's—all shot to hell.

MAGGIE. I'll keep in touch. (*He nods. She EXITS quickly. He moves to the phone, dials.*)

SCOTTIE. (*Into phone.*) Doctor Petrelli, please— How long ago did she leave?— No—no message. (*The energy drains out of him and he sits, staring ahead, dead-eyed. JUD appears on the balcony, a book in his hand. Although he tries to appear affable, there is an underlying hostility in his manner he can't quite disguise.*)

JUD. (*Finally.*) Mom gone?

SCOTTIE. Did we wake you?

JUD. No, I was reading. (SCOTTIE *nods, closes his eyes.* JUD *comes down the stairs, stands awkwardly, studying his father.*) Look—about last night. I guess I flew off the handle and said some—

SCOTTIE. Everything you said was true, Jud.

JUD. Then why did you let it happen?

SCOTTIE. A couple of years ago I was in England

and stopped in a wayside inn. On the menu they had a cheese sandwich and a ham sandwich. I asked the waitress if I could have a ham and cheese sandwich. She said (*Using Cockney accent.*), 'Oh, I don't know if I can do that, do I?' I suggested they simply combine the two sandwiches and I'd pay for both. 'Well, I'm going to 'ave to ask 'im, won't I?' She went off and had a lengthy discussion with the owner and then came back and said, 'No, he can't do it.' I asked why on earth not. 'He said if we do that who knows where it could all end.'

JUD. (*Puzzled.*) I don't understand why you told me that story.

SCOTTIE. All my life I've never given any thought to where any situation would all end. Last night I'm afraid I overdid it.

JUD. (*Edgily.*) Why is it that with you everything has to have a punch line?

SCOTTIE. (*Irritably.*) Because anybody can write the straight lines! Look, I'm very tired right now. We can talk about it later.

JUD. Let's just forget it. (*The DOORBELL rings. JUD moves towards front door, stops and turns.*) Look, is it okay if I stick around for the summer?

SCOTTIE. That's up to you, Jud. (*JUD opens the front door to reveal SALLY holding a deli bag with bagels and lox.*)

SALLY. Good morning, everybody! Nope . . . don't close the door. Listen, I have this fantastic offer. You get these fresh bagels and lox absolutely free. All you have to do in return is support me for the rest of my life. (*Sees SCOTTIE.*) Hey, you look terrible. What orgy were you at and why wasn't I invited?

SCOTTIE. You wouldn't have liked it anyway. Very badly organized . . . not enough coat hangers. As a matter of fact I spent the night with a bunch of old goats who were desperately trying to remember what an orgy was.

JUD. Do you ever see any of your dependents anymore?

SALLY. Dependents?

JUD. A bunch of out-of-work, deadbeat actors and directors he hired every time he got a show to produce. (*To* SCOTTIE.) Do you still see them?

SCOTTIE. Are you writing an article for your school paper?

JUD. I was just curious.

SCOTTIE. I try to keep in touch.

JUD. None of them had any talent, did they?

SCOTTIE. If you only choose friends who have talent, you're going to go through life very lonely.

JUD. But they always screwed up. I could never figure out why you kept hiring them.

SCOTTIE. (*A trifle tightly.*) Let's just say I was hedging my bets against heaven, okay? (*The DOOR-BELL rings.* SCOTTIE *rises.*) That's going to be business. Would you two children excuse me?

JUD. (*To* SALLY.) I'll help you get breakfast ready. (*They EXIT to kitchen.* SCOTTIE *opens the front door to reveal* DR. GLADYS PETRELLI.)

GLADYS. I want you to know I don't usually provide a pickup and delivery service. Are you all ready? You know my feet are still killing me?

SCOTTIE. I'm not going, Gladys.

GLADYS. Scottie, we went over all this last night. Let's not start again.

SCOTTIE. No, let's not. This time my decision is final.

GLADYS. Scottie, don't be stupid. We're talking about your *life*.

SCOTTIE. Exactly—and it's *my* life. (*As she goes to speak.*) As uncharacteristic as it may seem, let's discuss the quality of that life for a moment. You remember Joe Sapstead? Nice, funny, roly-poly guy with a face like the Campbell Soup kid? (*She nods.*) Well, he let them 'treat' him, and within two months, they'd reduced him to a stumbling, old man. Oh sure, he was alive—they said. But they never convinced me. Because I knew that wasn't him—that wasn't Joe.

GLADYS. That was a different case entirely. Joe Sapstead had a brain tumor.

SCOTTIE. What difference does that make? Can you promise me I'm not going to end up like that?

GLADYS. The only thing I can promise you is time.

SCOTTIE. Time for what? Gladys, I don't have an unfinished concerto. I'm not on the verge of a great discovery. I'm not even in the middle of a good anecdote.

GLADYS. Scottie, I'm not going to stand by and let you die.

SCOTTIE. You're determined to depress me, aren't you?

GLADYS. I'm trying to save you.

SCOTTIE. Give me a break, will ya? Look, I don't want to hang around and *bore* everyone to death. I mean, who wants to leave with the audience wanting less? Don't you understand, Gladys? I've lost all the prelims, maybe I'll be able to win the main event. (*He stops.*) Jesus, that line looked better in my head than it sounded.

GLADYS. (*Getting angry again.*) What the hell are you talking about? You think this is one of those dumb movies you wrote?

SCOTTIE. Now wait a minute—do I criticize *your* work?

GLADYS. What about your son?

SCOTTIE. (*Finally.*) Sometimes you have to cut your losses and run. (*She looks at him for a moment, sits.*)

GLADYS. How you feeling now?

SCOTTIE. Fine, just fine.

GLADYS. That won't last long.

SCOTTIE. You know, you used to be more fun.

GLADYS. Scottie, exactly what do you plan to do?

SCOTTIE. Try not to think about it.

GLADYS. Then what?

SCOTTIE. Make a nice, clean exit.

GLADYS. How?

SCOTTIE. Well, I was rather hoping you'd provide me with a handy little escape kit. (*She looks at him for a moment.*)

GLADYS. Scottie, I think it's about time someone told you there's a fine line between being a living legend and a horse's ass.

SCOTTIE. I hate it when you get philosophical.

GLADYS. It's not going to work this time.

SCOTTIE. What?

GLADYS. Using jokes to shut out reality.

SCOTTIE. (*Shrugs.*) Everybody uses something.

GLADYS. Yeah, but the morning after they have to come to grips with how it really is. You want to know how it really is with you, Scottie?

SCOTTIE. Of course not. (*As she goes to speak.*) Gladys, I'm not going to stand here and listen to you go over the boring, clinical story of the condition of my bone marrow. It defeats the whole purpose.

GLADYS. Don't do this to me, Scottie.

SCOTTIE. Look, Gladys, I have a great affection for you—my biggest regret is that you never officially adopted me—but I think it's about time I grew up and took charge of my own life.

GLADYS. Scottie, please . . .

SCOTTIE. The answer is no. No! (*He takes the blanket from the piano bench and starts up the stairs.*) Don't look so gloomy, Gladys. We can still date. (SCOTTIE *EXITS.* GLADYS *sits with her drink on the couch.* JUD *ENTERS with a tray of dishes from the kitchen.*)

JUD. Oh—hello, Doctor. You here to see Dad?

GLADYS. I was.

JUD. Oh?

GLADYS. Jud, do you know anything about your father's condition?

JUD. I know he's very ill.

GLADYS. Look, I don't have any time for niceties so—your father has a form of leukemia. It's very serious but it's treatable. If he starts treatment right now we have a good chance of prolonging his life—certainly months, possibly years. Last night when I saw him he agreed to go into the hospital this morning. Just now he did a complete about-face.

JUD. Did he say why?

GLADYS. He gave me some claptrap about not having anything important to stick around for. (JUD *is setting table for three.*)

JUD. Maybe it wasn't claptrap.

GLADYS. He has you.

JUD. That never stopped him from taking a walk before.

GLADYS. Jud, are you angry with your father for getting sick?

JUD. You're out of your class, Doctor. I've been analyzed by experts.

GLADYS. Did the two of you have some sort of disagreement?

JUD. It was a family matter.

GLADYS. What sort of family matter?

JUD. I don't think it's any of your business.

GLADYS. I'm not asking out of idle curiosity!

JUD. Look, I resent you barging in here and laying that sort of guilt upon me.

GLADYS. Then do something about it. Talk to him and convince him he has to change his mind.

JUD. Why me?

GLADYS. What do you mean, why you? You're the only important thing in his life.

JUD. You don't know my father as well as you think.

GLADYS. Talk to him, Jud.

JUD. I can't do that.

GLADYS. Why not?

JUD. He's a grown man. He obviously has his reasons. Anyway, there's nothing I could say that would change his mind!

GLADYS. (*Incredulously.*) And you don't think it's your responsibility to even *try?* (JUD *starts to speak but is interrupted when* SALLY *ENTERS from the kitchen carrying food and coffee.*)

SALLY. Oh—hi. I'm Sally Haines. You hungry?

GLADYS. No thanks—I was just leaving. Don't put it off too long, Jud. Do it this morning. (*She has crossed to the door.*)

JUD. Didn't you hear anything I've been saying?

GLADYS. When you think about it, you'll change your mind.

JUD. What makes you so sure?

GLADYS. Because when you stop defying people to like you I think you'll be a nice kid. I just know you can't be the selfish little prig you appear to be. (*She EXITS.*)

SALLY. Friend of yours? (JUD *is putting silverware at each place around the table.*) You want to tell me what just went on in here?

JUD. No.

SALLY. You have to.

JUD. Why?

SALLY. Because if we're going to be friends, I have to know why you're a selfish little prig.

JUD. Sally, knock it off, okay! (*He slams down remaining silver and crosses angrily to piano.*)

SALLY. Okay.

JUD. I'm sorry. I'm really—hassled this morning. I didn't mean to take it out on you. (*She looks at him.*)

SALLY. You know, if this thing between us is going to work out you're going to have to start kissing back.

JUD. Last night—after I left you—I walked in on my mother and father—together.

SALLY. (*Amused.*) You mean together or *together?* (*She realizes he is not amused.*) I'm sorry.

JUD. (*Tightly.*) Forget it, Sally. Just forget it.

SALLY. Why are you so uptight? What's a casual roll in the hay among old friends? You know how affectionate Scottie is.

JUD. (*Harshly.*) If he's so affectionate then why the hell did I stutter for five years!

SALLY. (*Finally.*) Didn't you ever like him, Jud?

JUD. Like him? I adored him. (*He shrugs.*) I mean, why not? It was like having an eight-year-old playmate as a permanent house guest.

SALLY. What happened?

JUD. He moved to a different neighborhood.

SALLY. It was a long time ago, Jud. Why are you so bitter?

JUD. You're right—it was a long time ago.

SALLY. You're doing it again. (*He looks at her for a moment, sits on the piano bench.*)

JUD. (*Finally.*) After the divorce, my father put in some token appearances, made a few phone calls and then put us on 'hold' for a few years. If you think I don't communicate now you should have seen me ten years ago. I was *not* easy to love. Then my mother met Don, my stepfather. He wanted to be my friend. At this point I wouldn't have accepted the friendship of *God*. But Don wouldn't give up—he just kept chipping away until he got to me.

He's a good man. It took a while—but after my mother married him I finally believed it was going to be permanent. It was the one thing in my life I could count on. Last night my father took care of that too.

SALLY. I don't get it. How's anyone going to find out about it? (*He looks at her for a moment.*)

JUD. (*Flatly.*) Jesus, you're just like him.

SALLY. Oh, come on, Jud, we'd all like to live neat, ordered, happy-ever-after lives but it just doesn't work out that way. Sometimes human impulses screw us up.

JUD. I don't understand that sort of morality. (*There is a pause.* SALLY *gets up.*)

SALLY. You know, I have a feeling we're never ever going to finish a meal together.

JUD. I can't be dishonest just because I want to go to bed with you.

SALLY. (*Wryly.*) Just my luck to get mixed up with an idealist. (*She gets her purse, moves towards the front door.*) You know our problem, Jud? You're too old for me. (*She turns at door, ruefully regards the food, looks at him.*) I doubt if we'll be seeing each other again but if we do, let's make a pact, huh? Eat first—talk later. (*She EXITS. After a moment,* JUD *softly picks out the melody of 'Scottie's Theme' with one finger. Suddenly, he starts furiously pounding out the song with both hands like a child just learning the piano. The angry, harsh playing builds to a climax.* LOU *ENTERS, stands listening until* JUD *in furious frustration slams the keyboard cover.*)

LOU. You okay, kid? (JUD *manages a nod.*) I didn't know you played.

JUD. My father's upstairs.

LOU. That's okay, it's you I wanted to see anyway. I wanted to talk to you about him.

JUD. You know about my father?

LOU. I suspected something was wrong a few weeks ago. (*He moves over to survey food.*) Then when he said he went to Vegas I didn't buy it for a moment. Gladys told me about the tests a couple of days ago.

JUD. (*Surprised.*) You knew when you were here yesterday?

LOU. Mind if I have some coffee?

JUD. I'm sorry about my father. I mean I know how close you two are.

LOU. Gladys phoned me this morning right after she left here.

JUD. I see.

LOU. (*Wearily.*) I don't. I don't understand why it had to hit Scottie, I don't understand why I lost my wife five years ago, I don't understand anything anymore. (*He looks at* JUD.) Mostly, I don't understand you.

JUD. (*Defensively.*) Look, he doesn't like pain—discomfort in any form. So why shouldn't he avoid it if he wants?

LOU. That explains him. What about you?

JUD. I respect his decision.

Lou. Suddenly you have respect?

Jud. Is my father good at his job? (Lou *looks at him*.)

Lou. What kind of question is that?

Jud. Is he?

Lou. Let me tell you about your father. He's a man who's misused his talent, he's avoided responsibility all his life, he's never been a fan of hard work, he's loused up every chance he ever had, he's squandered his money foolishly—and there's never been a time I didn't look forward to seeing him and I've never spent a moment with him that I wasn't amazed, amused or didn't thoroughly enjoy. And there are hundreds of people who feel just like me.

Jud. What you're saying is he's a crowd pleaser.

Lou. Exactly. And I wish to God we had a few more just like him.

Jud. Yes, well, somehow his charm escapes me.

Lou. That's because you're still young.

Jud. What's that got to do with anything?

Lou. Scottie reminds us of our lost childhood. Or maybe the childhood we never had. Look at me, Jud. I go to work, I put my kids through college— (*He shrugs*.) —I do my job. Like most people I live a meat and potatoes sort of life. But every now and then that guy dances into our lives, leads us astray and makes us remember the time when we didn't have to worry about mortgages or making a living or taking anything seriously.

Jud. There's got to be more to him than that.

Lou. Isn't that enough?

Jud. You don't think there's something sad about a man who never grew up? A man who never committed to anything worthwhile?

Lou. Worthwhile? You know, I've been thinking a

lot about your father the past couple of weeks. I think
he was blessed—or cursed—with never being able to
lose that extra something we all had to blot out very
early if we're going to function.

JUD. What's that?

LOU. The ability to stand back and realize the obvious—that absolutely nothing is that important.
Fortunately, he was also given the enormous gift for
taking a hamburger and making everyone around
him believe they were at a banquet. And if you think
that's not a good reason for living, there's something
wrong with your sense of values.

He's worth saving, Jud. (*The connection between
the two is shattered when, from the upstairs bedroom,
we hear a LOUD, EXPLOSIVE BANG that sounds
suspiciously like a GUNSHOT. The two freeze for a
moment before they are simultaneously galvanized
into action and make a dash for the stairs. They are
halfway up when they are stopped by the appearance
of* SCOTTIE *on the landing. He is wearing a fresh
change of clothes and is holding a recently-opened
magnum of champagne.*)

SCOTTIE. Cheers. (*He peers at* LOU's *face.*) Are you
okay, pal? You look quite odd.

LOU. I always look this way when my heart stops.
Scottie, what the hell are you doing?

SCOTTIE. Opening a bottle of champagne.

LOU. *Why?*

SCOTTIE. Well, I heard voices and I thought there
might be a party I was missing. (*Coming down
stairs.*) I always find that champagne and orange
juice make breakfast a little more festive.

LOU. Where'd you get it?

SCOTTIE. It's a gift from an old admirer in gratitude
for my sexual favors. That should tell you how old it
is. I'd stashed it away for a special occasion.

Lou. What's the special occasion this morning?

Scottie. The occasion is that I just opened a sixty-dollar bottle of champagne. (*Gives champagne and empty orange juice pitcher from bar to* Lou.) Now get some orange juice and ice while I round up a few of my favorite degenerates.

Lou. Champagne and orange juice coming right up. (*He EXITS to kitchen.* Scottie *takes the phone and his address book to the sofa and sits.*)

Jud. I need to talk to you, Dad?

Scottie. I think I've had enough scenes for one morning, Jud.

Jud. It can't wait.

Scottie. Yes, it can. I've found that I can avoid all emotional confrontations unless they're heavily under-scored by Dmitri Tiomkin.

Jud. (*A trifle bitterly.*) That must save you a lot of pain.

Scottie. (*Wearily.*) What is it, Jud?

Jud. I had a talk with Doctor Petrelli. (*There is a pause.*)

Scottie. Oh. (*A beat, lightly.*) She tell you about 'my body being all aching and racked with pain'?

Jud. No. Mom told me last night.

Scottie. I wish she hadn't done that.

Jud. Naturally, I was very sorry to hear the news.

Scottie. (*Quietly.*) Jesus, you sound like a Hall-mark card.

Jud. I'm sorry about that, too.

Scottie. Is that why you decided to stay?

Jud. It's one of the reasons.

Scottie. You don't have to, you know.

Jud. You're going to need all the help you can get.

Scottie. There's really nothing you can do.

Jud. For one thing, I can get you to the hospital. (Scottie *rises to face* Jud.)

SCOTTIE. Okay, you've made your token attempt. Now I'll say it once and then we'll forget it. I can't think of one good reason for me to change my mind.

JUD. I can. You owe it to me to stick around for as long as you can.

SCOTTIE. (*Coldly.*) I wasn't aware you held any of my unpaid markers. (*As* JUD *goes to speak.*) Look, maybe you were justified in your opinion of me last night but it didn't exactly fill me with paternal affection, so just get off my back, huh?

JUD. No. You've walked away from every responsibility you've ever had. Well, I'm not going to let you walk away from this one. (SCOTTIE *looks at him for a moment.*)

SCOTTIE. I see. And now you expect me to be suffused with guilt and atone by making some stupid, meaningless gesture.

JUD. It's for your benefit too, you know.

SCOTTIE. My benefit?

JUD. It might just give you some self-respect!

SCOTTIE. This may come as a great surprise to you but I am loaded with self-respect.

JUD. All right, then. Do it for me.

SCOTTIE. Why the hell should I?

JUD. Because I need you. When I needed you before you weren't there. Well, dammit, I need you *now!*

SCOTTIE. Where the hell were you when I needed *you?*

It's a two-way street, you know. I mean, where were you when I came back to New York and was beating my brains out trying to get a job? Even the past few years I haven't noticed you rushing down here to keep me company.

JUD. You never insisted I come.

SCOTTIE. That was your choice.

Jud. You shouldn't have given me a choice!

Scottie. Okay, let's just say I'm not the father you always wanted. Has it ever occurred to you that you're not the son I always wanted? Have you ever done one crazy, funny, spontaneous thing in your entire life? Have you ever even tried? (*There is a muffled banging on the door to the kitchen and* Lou's *voice.*)

Lou. (*OFFSTAGE.*) Can someone get this door?

Scottie. I'm going to tell you one thing, Jud—if that's not comedy relief we're both in a lot of trouble.

Jud. (*Angrily.*) Why don't you go fuck yourself! (*He turns, runs up the stairs and EXITS.* Scottie *looks after him.*)

Scottie. That's spontaneous—not very funny but it's spontaneous. (Scottie *opens kitchen door and* Lou *comes tripping in.*) You'd never get a job at the Savoy, Lou. (Lou *puts tray on table, starts to make drinks.*)

Lou. What happened to Jud?

Scottie. Good question.

Lou. (*Casually.*) You had a chance to talk to him this morning?

Scottie. Well, we don't really have talks. We have —interviews.

Lou. Interviews?

Scottie. Yes. It's the damnedest thing. All morning he's been asking these penetrating questions about my past.

Lou. What's the matter? You stuck for the answers?

Scottie. Well, it's rather like the classic student's nightmare where you're taking an exam and you know you haven't studied for it—I have this feeling I'm going to get a quiz on my life and the best I can hope for is a C−.

Lou. At last it's a passing grade. (SCOTTIE *turns to look at him.*)

SCOTTIE. Lou, how many times have I told you that you cannot go through life treating everything as a joke? (JUD, *carrying a suitcase, comes down the stairs, drops the suitcase in front of his father. Finally.*) Interesting prop.

JUD. It's yours. (*He dumps it on the floor between him and his father.*)

SCOTTIE. Oh?

JUD. You said I didn't hold any of your unpaid markers. Well, you have a bad memory—I came up with a few.

SCOTTIE. What is this going to accomplish, Jud?

JUD. We need some time.

SCOTTIE. Why?

JUD. I'm not ready to cry over you yet. (*THE TWO are staring at one another as the scrim comes in, the LIGHTS DIM and* MAGGIE *is illuminated by the Tribute SPOTLIGHT, DOWNSTAGE RIGHT.*)

MAGGIE. Scottie always loved people—the more the better. I remember some years ago, when we were married, it was *my* birthday and he suggested that he invite about a hundred friends over and throw me a big party. I said: 'Scottie, there's only one thing I want for my birthday. I'd like to have dinner with you—just you.' At first he didn't believe me but finally I convinced him. And so the two of us had a romantic dinner at home—all alone. At the end of the evening he gave me a perplexed look and said: 'This is what you really wanted?' I nodded. He kissed me and then said very tenderly: 'Well, to tell the truth, if you'd have asked *me* what I wanted on *my* birthday, I'd probably have said the same thing.' There was a long pause and he added: 'But I'd have been lying.' (*She looks around the theatre.*) Well, tonight looks like his kind of party so—happy birthday, Scottie! (*The SPOTLIGHT CROSS FADES to STAGE LEFT where* JUD *is standing.*)

JUD. During the past three months, I took close to two thousand photos of my father. I thought you might like to see some of them. (*The HIRSCHFELD drawing of* SCOTTIE *fades out as a series of slides is projected on the screen. The slides cover the three month period of the treatments prior to tonight's Tribute. They are underscored by a tape of* SCOTTIE'S *'Unfinished' played on the piano. When the slides are over the LIGHTS come up behind the scrim illuminating the apartment and we see* JUD *sitting with the earphones on projecting the slides on the fourth wall. After a moment he gets up to adjust the sound on the earphones. The audience does not hear the music but it does hear the DOORBELL and after a moment* SALLY *opens the front door and ENTERS. She is carrying a Bloomingdale's shopping bag and is all dressed for the Tribute. She taps* JUD *on the shoulder and he jumps, startled.*)

SALLY. I rang a couple of times, but no one answered.

JUD. Sorry. I was trying to select some music to go with the slides of my father.

SALLY. Find anything?

JUD. I can't make up my mind whether it should be the Hallelujah Chorus or Spike Jones. (*He goes to turn off projector.*)

SALLY. No, don't turn it off. I'd like to see them. Oh, that's nice. (*They continue to view slides until indicated.*) I suppose we should congratulate ourselves.

JUD. Why?

SALLY. The way we've managed to avoid each other these past three months. (*He glances at her.*)

JUD. Yes—well, I saw you a couple of times at the hospital but it was such a mob scene I didn't have a chance to talk to you.

SALLY. About what?

JUD. I wanted to apologize. I had no right to judge your life. (*She looks at him.*)

SALLY. You look tired, Jud.

JUD. Yes—well, this sort of experience tends to—mature a person.

SALLY. (*Indicating slide.*) I like that one. How is he today?

JUD. Okay. A bit testy because he thinks nobody's remembered it's his birthday.

SALLY. I've got his present right here. (*She goes to piano and picks up shopping bag which she brought in with her.*)

JUD. What did you get him?

SALLY. Another hat. What else?

JUD. Better not give it to him until tonight. If he knows we've remembered he might suspect we've planned something. (JUD *turns off projector.* SALLY *puts bag back on piano.*)

SALLY. How did you get the idea for the Tribute in the first place?

JUD. Well, his birthday was coming up and I thought a big party might be a nice gift.

SALLY. So you planned this whole thing on your own?

JUD. Well, Lou helped, too.

SALLY. I heard it was mostly you.

JUD. Yeah, well I've discovered there's a lot of Perle Mesta in me. (SCOTTIE *APPEARS on the landing. He is wearing a bright blonde Harpo Marx wig and carrying his jacket and tie.*)

SCOTTIE. Listen, I need your honest opinion. Do you think this tie goes with the suit?

SALLY. Perfect. But only if you carry a horn.

SCOTTIE. Do you happen to know the date, Sally?

SALLY. Uh— (*Gives today's date*). Why?

SCOTTIE. No reason. (*He EXITS into bedroom.*)

SALLY. He's exactly the same, isn't he? Only more so.

JUD. Yes. It's—amazing.

SALLY. Do you talk much about it?

JUD. Well, you know this place—we're not alone that much. (*He looks up, sees her studying him.*) I tried a couple of times but he didn't seem to want to and— (*He gives a little shrug.*) I admire him too much to invade his privacy.

SALLY. Oh?

JUD. (*Finally.*) Yes. I have great admiration for the way he's dealt with this whole thing. It must have been very rough for him but he never once complained—at least not to me.

SALLY. You two tied up your 'loose ends', huh? (*She sits beside* JUD.)

JUD. Well, I don't know— (*An attempt at lightness.*) —but I've used up a lot of film trying.

SALLY. Are you kidding?

JUD. No. I had this idea that by objectively studying the film I'd—well, I'd be able to bring him into focus. But you know my father—a 'master of disguise.'

Look, you use what you have. As you know—I've never been too great at—making contact.

SALLY. (*Moved.*) Oh, Jud, you don't have to reach out to Scottie. He has his arms out to the whole world.

JUD. I'm not the whole world. I'm his son.

SALLY. (*After a beat—gently.*) Look, I don't know

what really went on with you two but don't you think it's time to forgive him?

JUD. You can't forgive someone who isn't even aware he's done anything wrong.

SALLY. What do you want from him, Jud?

JUD. Something more. I don't know—maybe it's me.

SALLY. In what way?

JUD. (*Thoughtfully.*) Well, if you analyze it, (a) he doesn't love me enough to show me it, or (b) I don't love him enough to see it. (*After a moment, she leans forward and kisses him.*) My father may be right. I'm a very peculiar chap.

SALLY. Tell me about it.

JUD. All my life I'm going to regret I never got to know you better.

SALLY. (*Gently.*) Sure. I can just see you being interviewed when you're eighty-five—'I only have two regrets in my life, (a) I shouldn't have had the pastrami tonight, and (b) I should have boffed that model in 1978.'

JUD. It's entirely possible. (LOU, *looking rather harassed, ENTERS through the front door.*)

LOU. Can I talk?

JUD. He's upstairs.

LOU. Okay, everything's all set. I've been to the airport and back six times today. I got about fifty people stashed in hotels all over town. Oh, yeah, your mother checked into the Algonquin. She'll meet us at the theatre. Now I want you two to get out of here— (*Checking watch.*) —within fifteen minutes. (SCOTTIE, *now wearing a corduroy cap, APPEARS on the landing, starts down the stairs.*)

SCOTTIE. Where are my phone calls?

LOU. What?

SCOTTIE. Damnedest thing. For three months the

phone is ringing like I'm Truman Capote and then suddenly it stops. (LOU *crosses to the bar to make himself a drink.*)

LOU. Well, what do you expect? You doublecrossed everybody—you're still alive!

SCOTTIE. Doesn't anybody else find it cold in here? Quick, someone throw a hot starlet over me.

SALLY. I don't have a hot starlet but maybe this will do until the real thing comes along. (*She goes to* SCOTTIE. *and gives him a warm embrace.*)

SCOTTIE. Why are you all dressed up?

SALLY. Working duds. And I'm late.

SCOTTIE. Wait a minute—aren't you going to stay and play with me?

SALLY. I'd like to but I have to bring a little sunshine into the lives of five thousand Shriners.

SCOTTIE. What about me? Don't I get any sunshine?

SALLY. Sorry, Scottie, but the needy come first. (*She EXITS.*)

SCOTTIE. (*To* JUD.) If I were you, son, I'd hang onto that girl. Very tightly.

JUD. I know, I know. (JUD *is packing up his slide projector during the following.*)

SCOTTIE. You know, that damn phone hasn't been so quiet since I mistook Zanuck's wife for a hired party girl. You sure it isn't out of order?

LOU. I'll check. I want to make a few calls anyway. (*He EXITS to kitchen.* SCOTTIE *looks at* JUD *who is packing his projector into its case.*)

SCOTTIE. What time is your plane, son?

JUD. I'm taking the red eye.

SCOTTIE. I'm sorry it wasn't more fun for you, Jud.

JUD. I didn't stay because I was looking for fun.

SCOTTIE. Why did you stay?

JUD. I wanted to pay you back for all those **hours**

on the miniature golf course. (JUD *is taking his luggage from the bottom of the stairs and putting it by the front door.*)

SCOTTIE. Jud, when you were little, what the hell were you so sore about? I know the divorce was rough, but a lot of kids go through that and come out okay.

JUD. It—confused me. It took a long time to get straight in my head. Listen, I never was a quick study.

SCOTTIE. The separation?

JUD. It was a little more than that.

SCOTTIE. You have a captive audience.

JUD. It's not the sort of story that gets applause at the Friars' Club, Dad.

SCOTTIE. Well, you can't have me rolling in the aisles all the time.

JUD. Well, it wasn't a great traumatic event that shaped my life or anything. (JUD *sits at table LEFT and during the following is making a final check on his slides for the Tribute.*) It was just one of the reasons I was teed off at you for a few years. When I was about—oh, eight, I guess—we had a big party— it was at the house on Carmelina. Mom let me sleep in one of the bunks in the pool house—partly so the noise wouldn't keep me awake—partly as a special treat. I remember watching the lights from the pool rippling on the wooden ceiling as I drifted off to sleep. Later, I heard voices—yours and another—a woman —giggling and laughing. I was still half asleep and it took me a while to realize you were in the same room with me. Anyway, I watched you and the lady having sex.

'Having sex.' I mean, at the time I wasn't even sure that's what you were doing.

After a while, you both got up and left and I went

back to sleep. Six months later you and Mom split up and somehow in my addled little mind I tied in the whole incident with why you had to go away. It wasn't, of course. At least not that particular woman. (SCOTTIE, *very shaken, takes out a cigarette, searches for a match.* JUD *moves to him, lights his cigarette.*)

Look, as I said it was no great tragedy. Today, I could probably handle it but when you're eight years old you're saddled with a very old-fashioned sense of morality.

SCOTTIE. Jud, why didn't you ever tell me this before?

JUD. I was afraid you'd turn it into an amusing anecdote. (LOU *ENTERS from the kitchen with his usual handful of crumpled phone messages.*)

LOU. (*To* JUD.) Don't you have to pick up your airline ticket?

JUD. What?

LOU. Your airline ticket.

JUD. Oh—yeah. Listen, I'll see you later, Dad. Maybe we'll down a few beers and pick up a couple of chorus girls. Or should it be the other way around? (*He EXITS with box of slides.* SCOTTIE, *very shaken, sits, a strange, puzzled expression on his face.* LOU *is studying his phone messages.*)

LOU. So when you want to come back to work, kid? (*He looks up as* SCOTTIE *doesn't answer.*) Scottie, you okay? (SCOTTIE *speaks in a puzzled tone.*)

SCOTTIE. Jud just told me about something that happened when he was a kid. And you know what's crazy? I can't remember one thing about it. Isn't that the damnedest thing?

LOU. Yeah—well, they got a name for that. It's called 'age.'

SCOTTIE. How do you get along with your kids, Lou?

Lou. It varies. What the hell did Jud say to you?

Scottie. It wasn't only what he said—it was how. My God, it was like a lawyer delivering a brief. (Lou *decides to try and cheer him up, shoves messages into his pocket, crosses to bar to make himself a new drink.*)

Lou. Tell me, sir—how's your sex life?

Scottie. (*Absently falling for an old routine.*) Well, I could say it was meager, but I'd be bragging.

Lou. Why'd you break up with that last girlfriend? Speak right into the microphone.

Scottie. She was rotten.

Lou. What do you mean—rotten?

Scottie. I'll tell you how rotten she was. Whenever anyone in the world was rotten—she got a royalty. (Lou *laughs but it is obvious* Scottie *is not really with it.*)

Lou. What's the matter?

Scottie. I was just thinking—we started out as the Odd Couple and all of a sudden we turned into the Sunshine Boys.

Lou. (*Putting his drink on piano.*) If you're going to be depressing, I'm going.

Scottie. You're going to leave an old man with nothing to amuse him but his memories?

Lou. Get a grip on yourself, kid—nobody likes a whiner. I'll drop by later tonight and maybe we'll play some gin. (*He EXITS.*)

Scottie. Whoopee! (*He hums a few bars of 'Happy Birthday' as he stares at the phone. Finally he picks up the receiver and dials operator.*) Hello, operator— Hi there! Look, love, I'd like to report a serious malfunction in my phone— Well, I haven't had a call all morning— No, that's impossible. You see, I'm Scottie Templeton and although the name may not mean much to you, I'm an extremely popular fellow. You might say it's my life's work— Would you do that? It's 581-5610. (*He hangs up, waits. After a moment, the PHONE rings. He picks it up.*) How nice of you to call— Well, that's really odd and I must say it certainly makes me feel very insecure. You see, today happens to be my birthday— Ninety-one— Oh, yes, I'm a perfect physical specimen. What sort of physical shape are you in? (*The front DOORBELL rings.*) Listen, my love, can I call you back? There seems to be somebody at the front door. It's probably the naked Dixieland band I hired to cheer me up. (*He hangs up, crosses to the front door and opens it to reveal a woman of indeterminate age holding a suitcase in one hand and a small card in the other. She is wearing glasses and a white nurse's uniform, white hose and white orthopedic shoes.*)

NURSE. (*Peering at card.*) Mr. Scott Templeton?

SCOTTIE. That's right.

NURSE. Well, thank goodness for that— I tend to get lost. (*Entering.*) I'm your nurse. I'm sorry I'm late. Where shall I put my things?

SCOTTIE. Uh—hold it a minute. There must be some mistake. Who sent you? (*She puts suitcase down, takes off coat through following.*)

NURSE. Doctor Gladys Petrelli. She is your doctor, isn't she?

SCOTTIE. Yes, but I don't need a nurse.

NURSE. She said you did.

SCOTTIE. Well, she's wrong.

NURSE. (*Checks card again.*) You're Mr. Scott Templeton?

SCOTTIE. We've been all through that before. Look, do I look as if a need a nurse?

NURSE. I'm not qualified to give medical opinions.

She told me you'd need a practical nurse for six months.

SCOTTIE. For what?

NURSE. Whatever is necessary. Backrubs, bedpans, walks in the park—

SCOTTIE. Does she expect me to put on a bathrobe and a green eye shade and have you push me around in a wheelchair like Joseph Cotten?

NURSE. I didn't see that picture. I just go where she sends me.

SCOTTIE. Well, she sent you to the wrong place! (*He takes her bag to the front door. She sits by the hi-fi.*)

NURSE. You know, this really is too much.

SCOTTIE. I'm sorry.

NURSE. I really need this job. I'd counted on it. (*She begins to weep.*)

SCOTTIE. Oh, no!— Okay, take it easy. Maybe we can work something out.

NURSE. No. This is really humiliating. I'm a trained practical nurse. I shouldn't have—to beg. (*She is looking in her pockets.*) Do you have a kleenex? Mine are all balled up. (SCOTTIE *hands her his silk pocket handkerchief and she dabs her eyes.*) I'm sorry—this is ridiculous. Normally, I don't act like this but my husband is out of work . . . Well, you're not interested in my problems. Can this be laundered?

SCOTTIE. (*Taking handkerchief.*) Oh, forget it. Here, have a drink.

NURSE. I'm not supposed to drink when I'm on duty.

SCOTTIE. (*Pouring her a stiff drink of brandy.*) I won't tell if you won't. (*He hands her the drink.*) I'm sorry . . . I didn't mean to be testy before but I'm in a rotten mood today.

NURSE. Is it something to do with your condition?

SCOTTIE. No, it's nothing like that. (*He gives a little*

shrug.) It's just that it's my birthday and I seem to be the only one who's remembered.

NURSE. It's your birthday? (SCOTTIE *nods.*) Oh, if I'd known I'd have brought you something.

SCOTTIE. You would have done that?

NURSE. Oh, just something small—you know, a token gift like cookies or something.

SCOTTIE. Cookies . . . That's very sweet.

NURSE. Birthdays are very important. Maybe I could . . . no. (*She stands.*) Well, we'll just have to make do. (*She starts to unbutton the front of her dress.*)

SCOTTIE. I beg your pardon? (*She continues to undress.*)

NURSE. I warn you—it won't be much.

SCOTTIE. What—what are you doing?

NURSE. Look, don't think I do this for everyone— not even on their birthday.

SCOTTIE. (*Desperately.*) No— Listen, it's okay— I'll wait for the cookies! (*She is now in a half slip and a bra and is about to take off the bra.*) Seriously— Look, you have a job—you don't have to— (*He stops as he sees the two magnificent breasts in front of him. Slowly, recognition comes to his eyes.*) Hilary! That's Hilary! (*She takes off glasses and wig.*)

NURSE. (HILARY.) Well, I'm glad there are a couple of things about me you remember. Happy birthday, Scottie!

SCOTTIE. (*Looking at her breasts.*) Oh Hil—you shouldn't have. (*They embrace happily.* LOU, JUD *and* SALLY, *holding a tape recorder, burst onto the landing.*)

LOU. (*Coming down stairs.*) Put that girl down— you don't know where she's been.

SALLY. We got it all! We got it all on tape!

SCOTTIE. You remembered!

SALLY. Well, we thought you'd like her better than the ship with the clock in the middle.

LOU. And it's only the beginning. (*The* NURSE [HILARY] *moves to her case, gets dressed in the clothes we saw her wearing at the Tribute during following.* SCOTTIE *looks up at* JUD *who has remained on the landing.*)

SCOTTIE. Don't tell me you were in on this thing, too?

JUD. (*Dryly.*) Yeah, but first they made me promise I would phone the Vice Squad.

SALLY. It was all Lou's idea, but I provided the costume and the wig. Hilary brought everything else.

LOU. (*Moving towards door.*) Come on, we have a limo waiting outside.

JUD. I've got to get my camera. (JUD *EXITS upstairs.*)

LOU. We got something else planned that's going to knock you out of your seat!

HILARY. Hey! I need a little time to get changed.

SCOTTIE. You guys go ahead. I'll be right there.

LOU. What are you going to do?

SCOTTIE. It's my birthday. I got to stay and watch.

LOU. We're on a very tight schedule. (*To* HILARY.) Can you get into your clothes in five minutes? (*She looks at* SCOTTIE.)

HILARY. Is he kidding? (LOU *and* SALLY *EXIT.*)

SCOTTIE. Oldest gag in the book and I fell for it. You should have been an actress.

HILARY. Honey, I was.

SCOTTIE. (*Affectionately.*) I've missed you, my love.

HILARY. Not as much as I've missed you.

SCOTTIE. I bet you say that to all the boys.

HILARY. No, you'll always be my favorite john.

SCOTTIE. Come over here and give me a kiss—

(*Pointing to cheek.*) —here. (*She moves to kiss his cheek. At the last moment he turns his face, kisses her on the lips. They sit together on the sofa.*)

HILARY. How you holding up, kid? Gladys Petrelli told me you've been a bit under the weather.

SCOTTIE. (*Fakes puzzlement.*) Is that what she told you? Funny, she told *me* I had cancer. (*This breaks* HILARY *up. He joins in her laughter.*)

HILARY. Will you tell me why the hell we're laughing?

SCOTTIE. Listen, if you get any better ideas, let me know.

HILARY. But seriously.

SCOTTIE. Well, I'm not exactly the Student Prince at Heidelberg yet, but I'm getting there.

HILARY. Well, hang in there, kid. You never can tell. Look at me. (*He sits and watches her as she continues to change.*)

SCOTTIE. How is it with you?

HILARY. Oh, same old boring success story.

SCOTTIE. You don't miss the action?

HILARY. Well, let's not kid around—I miss the applause.

SCOTTIE. Lynn Fontanne says the same thing. You got yourself a fellow? (*She looks at him.*)

HILARY. Corny but true. (JUD *comes from upstairs with his camera. He leans against the railing RIGHT watching* HILARY *and his father.*)

SCOTTIE. Well, I hope he's a good clapper.

HILARY. And it's very sincere. (*She is getting into her dress.*)

SCOTTIE. It's like old times, isn't it? Do you know how many hours I've spent waiting for this lovely lady to get dressed?

HILARY. You were the best friend I ever had, Scottie.

Maybe the only one. (*She turns to look at him.*) You always treated me as a human being, never a hustler. I'll always remember that.

SCOTTIE. (*Shrugging it off.*) Everybody's a hustler in one way or another.

HILARY. Not you. I don't know how you did it—but somehow you managed to retain your amateur standing. Maybe you were hustling for something but nobody could figure out what it was. You want to know what I like best about you?

SCOTTIE. Maybe I should wait until your book comes out.

HILARY. You put out for everybody. You treat everybody exactly the same. (*He doesn't say anything.*) I mean it. It doesn't matter whether it's the doorman, your wife, your family, a movie star or a ten-dollar hooker. You give the same to everybody. That's really something. (*He is just staring at her.*) Don't be embarrassed—I wouldn't say it if it weren't true.

Scottie, you're a rare creature—a man with absolutely no order of priorities. (*She poses for him.*) So what do you think? Do I look respectable enough to escort you to the ball?

SCOTTIE. You look divine. Go ahead love, I'll be right there. (HILARY *EXITS.* JUD *crosses for* SCOTTIE's *coat.*) Jud, do you concur with Hilary's charming observation that I'm a man with no order of priorities?

JUD. She meant it as a compliment.

SCOTTIE. But you don't think it is.

JUD. Well, I guess I always wanted to be a priority.

SCOTTIE. Is that why you never really wanted to spend much time with me?

JUD. (*Holding* SCOTTIE's *coat for him.*) Dad, they're waiting.

SCOTTIE. Don't patronize me! Was that your reason?

JUD. Partly. Mostly I was jealous.

SCOTTIE. (*Puzzled.*) Of what?

JUD. Of you. I always felt like a clod around you. You said that I wasn't the son you wanted. Well, I always knew that.

SCOTTIE. Jud—

JUD. Oh, I wanted to be. Fantasy time. Anyway, a couple of years ago, I realized that I could never be like you.

SCOTTIE. That's where you're wrong. You're exactly like me. You never made an emotional commitment in your life, either. Don't look so stricken, son. You're still young. (*We hear a CAR HORN being honked outside.*) What's the matter? Does being a 'chip off the old block' scare you that much?

JUD. I don't know. I'm not sure who you are. (*The front door flies open to reveal an agitated HILARY.*)

HILARY. Scottie, if you don't get out of here soon, this damn thing's going to turn back into a pumpkin! (*JUD quickly EXITS. SCOTTIE stands a moment and as he turns to EXIT the LIGHTS DIM, the scrim comes in and the SPOTLIGHT picks up LOU DOWN-STAGE RIGHT at the Tribute.*)

LOU. Although you'd never know it by looking at us, Scottie and me are about the same age. Listen, go figure it. Anyway, for some reason he always brought out—the fatherly instinct in me. I guess he had that effect on a lot of people. (*His emotions barely under control.*) Well, I always knew he was fun to have around the house—but during the past months he's shown me he had something else going for him. The son-of-a-bitch has the guts of a lion. (*He gives a little shrug.*) Listen, I would have taken him just as he is but it's always nice when your kid grows up and makes you proud of him, too. (*He blows his nose to hide his emotion.*) Well—enough of that. Scottie Templeton, the man we've been talking about, has been sitting in the best seat in the house all evening listening to this replay of his life. And there he is. Scottie, stand up and take a bow. Give him a spot. Come on down. When we brought him to the theatre tonight he seemed completely stunned. It was probably the only time in his life I've seen him speechless. I'm not sure he's back to normal yet—I've been sneaking looks at him all evening and he still looks like a mural. But I'm sure he's recovered his powers of speech and I'm sure you'd all like to hear from him. Scottie. . . . (*A SPOTLIGHT illuminates* SCOTTIE *who is sitting in a box near the stage. He stands, looking oddly disoriented. He stares around the theatre and then, as* LOU *beckons to him from the stage, he moves slowly down the few steps that lead from the box to the stage. He crosses to* DOWN CENTER *and* LOU *EXITS, leaving* SCOTTIE *alone on the stage. He looks out at the audience for a long moment, shakes his head, gives an incredulous chuckle.*)

SCOTTIE. (*Finally.*) Yes, but will you still respect me in the morning? (*He pauses, grins, and looks around the theatre.*) Okay, that ends the formal part of my lecture. Now for the question and answer period. (*He shakes his head, manages a chuckle.*) This has been quite a night. I've been listening to all those funny, charming stories about me. Lot of laughs! (*He pauses, thinks for a moment.*) I had an aunt who used to think she was a poached egg. It's true. Oh, not all the time—just on odd days. She used to carry this small brown mat around with her. That was her toast. She'd sit in the middle of it and nobody was allowed to step on her toast. I suppose it was her way of making sure that nobody ever got too close to her. (*A beat.*) Well, it seems as if all my life I've been carrying my own brown mat around with me. (*A beat.*)

You are my friends and you are the greatest audience anyone could ask for. (*He trails off, clears his throat.*) Actually, I'd like to take this time to have a chat with my son. I know that seems a little—peculiar—but— (*He grins.*) I've always been more comfortable with large groups. So if you're still out there, Jud— (*Awkwardly.*) We don't know each other very well—but that's not your fault. I never let anyone know me. (*A beat.*) A few months ago I had this crazy idea that I'd like to leave you with something. Well, tonight, as I listened I realized what it was I should really try to pass on to you. (*A pause.*) If I could wish one thing for you, Jud, it's a passion—for anything—anybody— that will go the distance. (*A beat.*) I never had the strength to fail with you. I just never laid anything on the line. I missed so much . . . (*A pause.*) Uh—now let me make a confession. You see before you a man who has absolutely no finish for this. (*A pause.*) Okay, here's the punch line. (*He thinks.*) There is no punch line. (*Another pause.*) I'm not kidding. I don't know how to get off. (*He grins foolishly, looks around, clears his throat.*) Well— (*He stops. There is a moment's tense silence before we hear a loud, strained VOICE from the back of the theatre.*)

JUD. (*Stuttering slightly.*) What about that girl you had in Pennsylvania?

SCOTTIE. (*Vaguely.*) What?

JUD. What about that girl you had in Pennsylvania? (SCOTTIE *peers out and we see* JUD *coming down the aisle, his eyes fixed on his father. He stops halfway down the aisle.*)

SCOTTIE. (*Weakly.*) Erie?

JUD. Well, I had to admit she was a little weird. And what about your brother in Alaska? (*The two are staring at one another, unsmiling.*)

SCOTTIE. Nome?

JUD. (*Moving down to in FRONT OF STAGE.*)
Of course I know'm. He's my uncle. The cat. . . .
(SCOTTIE *is just staring at him.*)

SCOTTIE. What?

JUD. The cat? (SCOTTIE *looks at him, puzzled.*)

SCOTTIE. I'm sorry—I'm not used to playing straight
man. Did you put out the cat?

JUD. Why? Was he on fire? (SCOTTIE *doesn't say
anything for a long moment.*)

SCOTTIE. (*Finally.*) Come up here and give me a
kiss— (*He points to his cheek.*) —here. (*After a moment,* JUD *moves up on the stage and crosses to*
SCOTTIE *to kiss him on the cheek where he has indicated. At the last moment* SCOTTIE *turns his face and
kisses him on the mouth. The two embrace and cling
tightly to one another. They break and look at one
another. They stand for a long moment before* SCOTTIE
reaches out to tousle JUD's *hair in a fatherly gesture,
puts his arms around his shoulder and the two move
slowly OFFSTAGE. As they do,* SCOTTIE's *trousers
slowly slip down to around his ankles and he waddles
off as the LIGHTS SLOWLY DIM until the stage
is in DARKNESS and the play is over.*)

THE END

PROPERTY PLOT

One-half hour—brew 12 cups coffee in percolator
(one-third in thermos, one-third in ceramic pot)

<small>PRESET ONSTAGE</small>—Drapes Open

Dining Table:
    silver cigarette urn (with cigarettes)
    large stone ashtray
    matches
    2 chairs

Left of Sofa:
    cigarette box
    matches

Sofa:
    4 pillows

Coffee Table:
    silver cigarette urn (with cigarettes)
    small stone ashtray

Bookshelf:
    loose mail

Telephone Shelf:
    telephone (off hook)
    memo pad
    pencil
    address book

Piano:
    several framed photographs, one of Jud
    pewter cigarette urn (with cigarettes)
    glass ashtray
    lighter
    matches

Shelf:
    hi-fi

headphones (upstage of hi-fi)
3 pillows
typewriter
Mantel:
photo album
Bar—
  Top Shelf:
    3 tumblers
    1 sour glass
    4 small brandy snifters
    2 champagne glasses
  Middle Shelf:
    1 tumbler
    4 sour glasses
    2 large brandy snifters
    1 juice glass
    pile of cocktail napkins
    orange juice pitcher (full)
    glass cigarette urn (with cigarettes)
    lighter
    matches
  Bottom Shelf:
    Bloody Mary mix bottle
    scotch bottle (with pourer)
    vodka bottle (with pourer)
    brandy bottle (with pourer)
    stirrer
    ice bucket (with ice)
    soda syphon
PRESET OFFSTAGE—
  Kitchen:
    2 juice glasses on bottom shelf in open cupboard
    pink memo pad (for Lou)
    empty orange juice pitcher
    extra cup (for Lou)

stirrer
round plastic tray:
  ceramic pot
  2 cups
  2 spoons
  glass sugar
  glass creamer
steel tray:
  thermos
  2 cups
  2 spoons
  stoneware sugar
  stoneware creamer
silver tray (under counter):
  3 cups
  3 juice glasses
  3 knives
  3 forks
  3 spoons
  3 napkins
  3 plates
  3 placemats (top)
Upstairs:
  Sally's bag
  Scottie's leather bag
  glass ashtray
  champagne bottle
  blonde wig
  Jud's book
  tape recorder
  auto robe
  loaded starter pistol } (for champagne-opening
  asbestos lined pad   }   sound effect)
Prop Table:
  Maggie's bag

Gladys' briefcase
Jud's luggage:
metal suitcase
  canvas bag
  duffel bag
  camera bag
  (empty) projector case
camera
camera case
film container (with film inside)
pink memo pad
pencil
shopping bag (with present inside)
Hilary's suitcase
white paper bag (with bagels & fake lox inside)
breakfast tray:
  3 bagels
  lox & cream cheese (set at intermission under
  counter)
empty open carousel box (with box of slides)
projector (with lens out: AC cord remote control
  and lid on top)
carousel on projector
blanket
picnic bag:
  2 sandwiches
  2 paper plates
  2 napkins
  jar with pickles
  cookie box
  potato salad carton
  full wine bottle

SCENE CHANGES

Act One, Scene 1 to Act One, Scene 2
  Set—
    picnic bag stage left of ottoman
    Jud's jacket to front door hook
  Strike—
    tray from piano (leave ceramic pot in kitchen
      with remaining coffee)
    move camera bag from prop table to upstairs
    put camera in case on upstairs hook
Act One, Scene 2 to Act One, Scene 3
  Strike—
    glasses from coffee table
  Intermission—
  Set—
    empty pitcher on bar
    blanket on sofa
    close drapes
   lox & cream cheese on bagel tray under counter
  Strike—
    wine bottle & glass from piano
    full orange juice pitcher from bar to kitchen
    picnic bag
    photo album
    auto robe
    top page of memo pad
    all used cups & glasses
    empty ashtrays
    move duffel bag from upstairs to prop table
Act Two, Scene 1 to Act Two, Scene 2
  Set—
    Jud's luggage to right rail:
      metal suitcase
      canvas bag

duffel bag

open projector case

headphones to top step

phone, pad, pencil, address book right of sofa

projector on phone shelf (with lid against rail)

carousel box on 1st step down

close drapes

Strike—

everything on dining table (except matches, urn & ashtray)

all used glasses & cups

book from piano

Jud's raincoat from front door hook

Scottie's suitcase from sofa